U0025479

The Canterville Ghost

鬼當家

原著 Oscar Wilde

改寫 David A. Hill

譯者 安卡斯

ABOUT THIS BOOK

For the Student

 Listen to the story and do some activities on your Audio CD.

 Talk about the story.

For the Teacher

Go to our Readers Resource site for information on using readers and downloadable Resource Sheets, photocopiable Worksheets, and Tapescripts. www.helblingreaders.com

For lots of great ideas on using Graded Readers consult Reading Matters, the Teacher's Guide to using Helbling Readers.

Structures

Modal verb would	Non-defining relative clauses
I'd love to . . .	Present perfect continuous
Future continuous	Used to / would
Present perfect future	Used to / used to doing
Reported speech / verbs / questions	Second conditional
Past perfect	Expressing wishes and regrets
Defining relative clauses	

Structures from other levels are also included.

CONTENTS

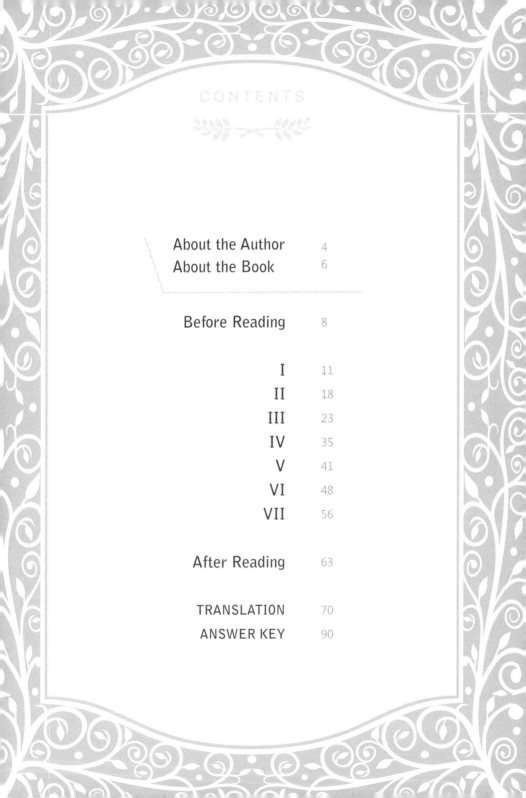

ABOUT THE AUTHOR

Oscar Wilde was born in Dublin in 1854, the son of an eminent[1] surgeon and a poet-cum-literary hostess. After reading classics at Dublin, Wilde went to Magdelen College, Oxford, where he won a poetry prize and gathered a wide circle of admirers.

His first book, *Poems*, was published in 1881. In 1884 he married Constance Lloyd and he wrote the charming fairy tales that became the highly successful *The Happy Prince and Other Tales* for their sons.

Then, after two years of working as a journal editor, Wilde returned to the literary circles in which his sparkling wit[2] was better appreciated. His novel *The Picture of Dorian Gray* was published in 1890 but the low morals of its protagonist shocked the Victorian public.

A year later, *Lord Arthur Savile's Crime and Other Stories* was published; it contained 'The Canterville Ghost'. Wilde became famous with his plays *Lady Windermere's Fan* (1892), *A Woman of No Importance* (1893), *An Ideal Husband* (1895) and *The Importance of Being Earnest* (1895). They lampooned[3] the morals and taboos[4] of Victorian society, and exposed its hypocrisies, with a highly successful blend[5] of humor and sharp wit.

However, in 1895, the Marquess of Queensberry, father of Wilde's close friend, Lord Alfred Douglas, publicly accused Wilde of seducing his son. Wilde sued Queensberry for libel[6], but Queensberry won and Wilde was sentenced to two years in prison.

While in prison, he wrote *De Profundis*, published posthumously[7], and *The Ballad of Reading Gaol* (1898) portraying the horrors of prison. After his release, he became bankrupt and he fell ill, both physically and mentally. He moved abroad and died in Paris in 1900.

---

1 eminent [ˈɛmənənt] (a.) 出色的
2 wit [wɪt] (n.) 機智
3 lampoon [læmˈpun] (v.) 作詩文諷刺
4 taboo [təˈbu] (n.) 禁忌
5 blend [blɛnd] (n.) 融合
6 libel [ˈlaɪbl̩] (n.) 誹謗
7 posthumously [ˈpɑstʃəməslɪ] (adv.) 於死後

ABOUT THE BOOK

The Canterville Ghost appeared in book form in 1891, in a collection of stories for adults called *Lord Arthur Savile's Crime and Other Stories*. It contained six new stories, plus two of his most popular children's stories ('The Happy Prince', and 'The Devoted Friend').

The story is about the Otises – an American family who buy an old house from Lord Canterville, an English aristocrat. The house has been haunted[1] by the ghost of Sir Simon de Canterville for 300 years. The Americans do not believe in the ghost at first, and when he appears they take an amused and pragmatic[2] view of him, refusing to be scared. This depresses the ghost, who is frustrated at not being able to do his work properly[3]. Eventually, the ghost is allowed to 'die' thanks to the kindness of Virginia Otis, the daughter of the family.

Ghost stories were very popular in Victorian England, with many major writers producing them, including Charles Dickens, Anthony Trollope, and William Collins. Wilde, however, uses the ghost-story format in an unconventional way. We feel sorry for the ghost instead of being afraid of him. Wilde also uses the story to make fun of both the British aristocracy and their traditions and conventions, and the Americans with their straightforward[4], no-nonsense view of the world, and their sense of superiority to the British. There are many amusing comments made on this topic[5].

The story also illustrates Wilde's ideas on beauty. The story is very sensuous, and includes some lovely detailed descriptions, and it also reflects his belief that the power of beauty can make things better, with the beautiful Virginia triumphing[6] over the evil of the ghost.

The love story between Virginia and Duke of Cheshire is a typical piece of Victorian sentimental writing, and the plot could be described as being melodramatic; however the charm and humor of the central ghost-story theme, combined with Wilde's characteristic satire[7], transform this short story into a powerful and evocative[8] tale.

1 haunt [hɔnt] (v.) 鬧鬼
2 pragmatic [præɡˋmætɪk] (a.) 務實的
3 properly [ˋprɑpəlɪ] (adv.) 正確地
4 straightforward [ˌstretˋfɔrwəd] (a.) 直截的；簡單的
5 topic [ˋtɑpɪk] (n.) 話題；主題
6 triumph [ˋtraɪəmf] (v.) 獲得勝利
7 satire [ˋsætaɪr] (n.) 諷刺作品
8 evocative [ɪˋvɑkətɪv] (a.) 喚起感情的

A Ghosts and the supernatural

1 What is a ghost? Write your own definition, then get into groups and share your ideas to write a group definition.

2 Do you believe in ghosts? Why/why not?

3 What sort of things are ghosts supposed to do? Look at the verbs in the box below and write sentences using these words to give examples of ghosts' behavior. Use a dictionary to help you, if necessary.

APPEAR	CLANK	CRY	FRIGHTEN	GROAN
HAUNT	RATTLE	SCARE	SHRIEK	VANISH

4 What do ghosts look like? Write a description of a ghost.

5 What stories have you read and what films have you seen with ghosts as the main characters? Choose the one you liked most or can remember best, and write a summary of the plot.

❸ The Americans and the British

6 What differences do you think there are between the American and the British people? Make a list. Write words you associate with each nation.

_____   _____

_____   _____

_____   _____

_____   _____

7 How different is the English spoken in Britain to that spoken in America? Tick US or UK for the words below.

	US	UK
a candy	☐	☐
b elevator	☐	☐
c gas	☐	☐
d handbag	☐	☐
e lift	☐	☐
f pants	☐	☐
g pavement	☐	☐
h petrol	☐	☐

8 How are some words spelt differently in British and American English? Rewrite the following words with a British English spelling. What are the rules for spelling?

a color _____

b center _____

c program _____

d traveling _____

When Mr Hiram B. Otis, the American Minister[1], bought Canterville Chase[2], everyone told him he was doing a very foolish thing, as there was no doubt at all that the place was haunted. Indeed, Lord Canterville himself, who was a man of absolute honor, had felt it his duty to mention[3] the fact to Mr Otis, when they came to discuss terms.

'We have not cared to live in the place ourselves,' said Lord Canterville, 'since my grand aunt, the Duchess of Bolton, was frightened into a fit[4] from which she never really recovered, by two skeleton hands being placed on her shoulders as she was dressing for dinner; and I feel bound[5] to tell you, Mr Otis, that the ghost has been seen by several living members of my family, as well as by the rector[6] of the parish[7], the Rev.[8] Augustus Dampier. After the unfortunate accident to the Duchess, none of our younger servants would stay with us, and Lady Canterville often got very little sleep at night, because of the mysterious noises that came from the corridor and the library.'

---

1 minister [ˈmɪnɪstə] (n.) 外交使節
2 chase [tʃes] (n.) 狩獵地；獵場
3 mention [ˈmɛnʃən] (v.) 提及
4 fit [fɪt] (n.) 痙攣或抽搐的突然發作
5 bound to [baʊnd tu] 一定會（做）

6 rector [ˈrɛktə] (n.) 教區牧師
7 parish [ˈpærɪʃ] (n.) 教區
8 Reverend [ˈrɛvərənd] (n.) 牧師
（縮寫 Rev.）

'My Lord,' answered the Minister, 'I will take the furniture and the ghost at a valuation. I come from a modern country, where we have everything money can buy; and with all our young men painting Europe red[1], and carrying off[2] your best actresses and prima-donnas[3], I reckon[4] that if there were such a thing as a ghost in Europe, we'd have it at home in a very short time in one of our public museums, or on the road as a show.'

'I fear that the ghost exists,' said Lord Canterville, smiling, 'though it may have resisted your enterprising[5] impresarios[6]. It has been well known for three centuries (since 1584, in fact), and always makes its appearance before the death of any member of our family.'

'Well, so does the family doctor for that matter, Lord Canterville. But there is no such thing, sir, as a ghost.'

'If you don't mind a ghost in the house, it is all right," answered Lord Canterville. 'Only you must remember I warned you.'

Mr Otis

- Why do you think that Mr Otis doesn't believe in the ghost?
- Do you believe in ghosts?

A few weeks after this, the purchase was completed, and the Minister and his family went down to Canterville Chase. Mrs Otis, who, as Miss Lucretia R. Tappan, of West 53rd Street, had been a celebrated New York belle[7], was now a very handsome middle-aged woman, with fine eyes, and a superb[8] profile[9]. She was in very good health, and had a really wonderful amount of animal spirits. Indeed, in many ways, she was quite English, and was an excellent example of the fact that we really have everything in common with America nowadays, except, of course, language.

Her eldest son, christened[10] Washington by his parents in a moment of patriotism (which he never ceased to regret), was a fair-haired, rather good-looking young man, and in London was well known as an excellent dancer. Gardenias[11] and English nobility were his only weaknesses. Otherwise he was extremely sensible[12].

Miss Virginia E. Otis was a little girl of fifteen, lithe[13] and lovely, and with a fine freedom in her large blue eyes. After Virginia came the twins, who were delightful boys.

---

1 paint Europe red〔俚〕在歐
    洲玩得很盡興
2 carry off 帶走
3 prima-donna [ˌprimə`dɑnə]
    (n.) 首席女歌伶
4 reckon [`rɛkən] (v.)〔口〕猜想
5 enterprising [`ɛntə·ˌpraɪzɪŋ] (a.)
    有事業心的

6 impresario [ˌɪmprɪ`sɑrɪˌo] (n.)
    （歌劇或演奏會）經理人
7 belle [bɛl] (n.) 美女
8 superb [su`pɝb] (a.) 高雅的
9 profile [`profaɪl] (n.) 輪廓；外形
10 christen [`krɪsn̩] (v.) 命名
11 gardenia [gɑr`dinɪə] (n.) 梔子花
12 sensible [`sɛnsəbl̩] (a.) 明理的
13 lithe [laɪð] (a.) 輕盈的

As Canterville Chase is seven miles from Ascot, the nearest railway station, Mr Otis had telegraphed for a horse and carriage to meet them, and they started their drive in high spirits.

It was a lovely July evening, and the air was delicate with the scent of pinewoods. Now and then they heard a wood pigeon or saw a pheasant. Little squirrels looked at them from the beech trees as they went by, and the rabbits ran away into the bushes with their white tails in the air.

As they entered the avenue of Canterville Chase, however, the sky became suddenly overcast[1] with clouds, a curious stillness seemed to hold the atmosphere, and, before they reached the house, some big drops of rain had fallen.

Standing on the steps to receive them was an old woman, neatly dressed in black silk, with a white cap and apron. This was Mrs Umney, the housekeeper. 'I bid[2] you welcome to Canterville Chase,' she said in an old-fashioned way.

Following her, they passed through the Tudor hall into the library, a long, low room, paneled in black oak[3], at the end of which was a large stained-glass[4] window. Here they found tea laid out[5] for them, and they sat down and began to look around while Mrs Umney waited on[6] them.

Suddenly Mrs Otis caught sight of a dull red mark on the floor just by the fireplace and, quite unconscious of what it really meant, said to Mrs Umney, 'I'm afraid something has been spilt there.'

'Yes, madam,' replied the old housekeeper in a low voice, 'blood has been spilt on that spot.'

---

1 overcast ['ovɚ,kæst] (a.)
　（雲）遮蔽（天空）的
2 bid [bɪd] (v.) 向……表示
3 oak [ok] (n.) 橡樹

4 stained-glass ['stend'glæs]
　(n.) 彩繪玻璃
5 lay out 擺設
6 wait on 伺候

'How horrid[1],' cried Mrs Otis; 'I don't care for blood-stains[2] in a sitting-room. It must be removed at once.'

The old woman smiled, and answered in a low, mysterious voice: 'It is the blood of Lady Eleanore de Canterville, who was murdered on that very spot by her husband, Sir Simon de Canterville, in 1572. Sir Simon survived her by nine years, and disappeared suddenly in very mysterious circumstances. His body has never been discovered, but his guilty spirit still haunts the Chase. The blood-stain has been much admired by tourists and others, and cannot be removed.'

'That is all nonsense,' cried Washington Otis; 'Pinkerton's Champion Stain Remover[3] and Paragon Detergent[4] will clean it up in no time,' and before the terrified housekeeper could interfere he had fallen upon his knees, and was rapidly scouring[5] the floor with a small stick of what looked like a black cosmetic. In a few moments no trace[6] of the blood-stain could be seen.

'I knew Pinkerton would do it,' he exclaimed triumphantly, as he looked round at his admiring family; but no sooner had he said these words than a terrible flash of lightning lit up the dark room, a frightening clap of thunder made them all jump to their feet, and Mrs Umney fainted[7].

'What an awful climate!' said the American Minister calmly, as he lit a long cigar. 'I guess the old country is so overpopulated that they don't have enough decent weather for everybody.'

'My dear Hiram,' cried Mrs Otis, 'what can we do with a woman who faints?'

'Make her pay every time she does it, as with anything she breaks,' answered the Minister; 'she won't faint after that.'

In a few moments Mrs Umney came to⁸. There was no doubt, however, that she was extremely upset, and she warned Mr Otis to beware of some trouble coming to the house.

'I have seen things with my own eyes, sir,' she said, 'that would make a Christian's hair stand on end, and many and many a night I have not closed my eyes in sleep for the awful things that are done here.'

Mr Otis, however, and his wife warmly assured the honest servant that they were not afraid of ghosts, and, after asking Providence⁹ to bless her new master and mistress, and making arrangements for an increase in salary, the old housekeeper went off to her own room.

Atmosphere

- What kind of atmosphere surrounds Canterville Chase?
- Does the weather usually affect the way you feel?

1 horrid [ˈhɔrɪd] (a.) 可怕的
2 blood-stain [ˈblʌdˌsten] (n.) 血跡
3 remover [rɪˈmuvɚ] (n.) 去除劑
4 detergent [dɪˈtɝdʒənt] (n.) 清潔劑
5 scour [skaur] (v.) 擦淨

6 trace [tres] (n.) 痕跡
7 faint [fent] (v.) 昏厥
8 came to 甦醒過來
9 Providence [ˈprɑvədəns] (n.)（大寫）上帝

The storm raged[1] fiercely all that night, but nothing of particular note[2] happened. The next morning, however, when they came down to breakfast, they found the terrible stain of blood once again on the floor.

'I don't think it can be the fault of the Paragon Detergent,' said Washington, 'for I have tried it with everything. It must be the ghost.'

He then rubbed out the stain a second time, but the second morning it appeared again.

The third morning also it was there, though the library had been locked up at night by Mr Otis himself, and the key carried upstairs.

The whole family were now quite interested; Mr Otis began to suspect that he had been too dogmatic[3] in his denial of the existence of ghosts, and Mrs Otis expressed her intention of joining a Psychical[4] Society[5]. That night all doubts about the actual existence of phantoms were removed for ever.

The day had been warm and sunny; and in the cool of the evening, the whole family went out for a drive. They did not return home till nine o'clock, when they had a light supper. The conversation in no way included a discussion of ghosts, so there were not even the right conditions of receptive[6] expectation[7] which so often precede psychical phenomena.

No mention at all was made of the supernatural, nor was Sir Simon de Canterville mentioned in any way. At eleven o'clock the family went to bed and by half past eleven all the lights were out. Some time after, Mr Otis was awakened by a curious noise in the corridor, outside his room. It sounded like the clank[8] of metal, and seemed to be coming nearer every moment.

He got up at once, struck a match, and looked at the time. It was exactly one o'clock. He was quite calm, and felt his pulse[9], which was not at all feverish. The strange noise still continued, and with it he heard the distinct sound of footsteps. He put on his slippers, took a small glass bottle out of a drawer, and opened the door.

Right in front of him he saw, in the pale moonlight, an old man of terrible appearance. His eyes were as red as burning coals; his long grey hair fell over his shoulders in greasy curls; his clothes, which were of an ancient style, were dirty and ragged[10], and from his wrists and ankles hung heavy manacles[11] and rusty chains.

'My dear sir,' said Mr Otis, 'I really must insist on your oiling those chains, and have brought you for that purpose a small bottle of Tammany Rising Sun Lubricator[12]. They say it works at once. I shall leave it here for you by the bedroom candles, and will be happy to supply you with more should you require it.'

1 rage [redʒ] (v.) 肆虐
2 note [not] (n.) 重要性
3 dogmatic [dɔgˋmætɪk] (a.) 教條的
4 psychical [ˋsaɪkɪkl̩] (a.) 靈魂的
5 society [səˋsaɪətɪ] (n.) 社團；協會
6 receptive [rɪˋsɛptɪv] (a.) 能接受的
7 expectation [ˌɛkspɛkˋteʃən] (n.) 期待
8 clank [klæŋk] (n.) 噹啷聲
9 pulse [pʌls] (n.) 脈搏；脈動
10 ragged [ˋrægɪd] (a.) 衣衫襤褸的
11 manacles [ˋmænəkl̩z] (n.) （複數形）手銬；腳鐐
12 lubricator [ˋlubrɪˌketɚ] (n.) 潤滑劑

With these words the United States Minister laid the bottle down on a marble[1] table, and, closing his door, went back to bed.

For a moment the Canterville ghost stood quite motionless in natural indignation[2]; then, knocking the bottle violently onto the polished[3] floor, he ran down the corridor, groaning and giving out a ghastly[4] green light. Just, however, as he reached the top of the great oak staircase, a door was thrown open[5], two little figures appeared, and a large pillow flew past his head! There was evidently no time to be lost, so, quickly using the Fourth Dimension of Space as a means of escape, he vanished through the wall, and the house became completely quiet.

On reaching a small secret chamber[6] in the left wing[7] of the house, he leaned up against a moonbeam[8] to recover his breath, and began to try and understand his position. Never, in a brilliant career of three hundred years, had he been so badly insulted.

The Canterville Ghost

- What is Mr Otis's reaction to the ghost and how does the ghost feel about this?
- Who do you think the 'two little figures' are?
- How does the ghost escape?

1 marble ['mɑrbl] (a.) 大理石的
2 indignation [ˌɪndɪɡ'neʃən] (n.) 憤怒；憤慨
3 polished ['pɑlɪʃt] (a.) 擦亮的
4 ghastly ['ɡæstlɪ] (a.) 恐怖的
5 throw open 突然大大地被打開
6 chamber ['tʃembɚ] (n.) 房間
7 wing [wɪŋ] (n.) 側廳；廂房
8 moonbeam ['mun,bim] (n.) 月光

He thought of the Duchess, whom he had frightened into a fit as she stood before the mirror in her lace and diamonds; of the four housemaids, who had gone off into hysterics[1] when he just grinned[2] at them through the curtains of one of the spare[3] bedrooms; of the priest whose candle he had blown out as he was coming late one night from the library, and who was still being treated for a nervous disorder; and of old Madame de Tremouillac, who, having wakened up one morning early and seen a skeleton seated in an arm-chair by the fire reading her diary, had been confined[4] to her bed for six weeks with an attack of brain fever.

He remembered the terrible night when the wicked Lord Canterville was found choking[5] in his dressing-room with a card half-way down his throat, and confessed, just before he died, that he had cheated Charles James Fox out of £50,000 while they were playing cards, and swore that the ghost had made him swallow it.

All his great achievements came back to him again, from the manservant who had shot himself because he had seen a green hand knocking at the window, to the beautiful Lady Stutfield, who always wore a black velvet band round her throat to hide the mark of five fingers burnt upon her white skin, and who drowned[6] herself in the fish-pond in the garden.

With the enthusiasm of a true artist, he went over his most celebrated performances. And after all this, some wretched[7] modern Americans had come and offered him the Rising Sun Lubricator, and thrown pillows at his head. It was quite unbearable! Besides, no ghosts in history had been treated in this way. So, he decided to have revenge[8], and remained till daylight deep in thought.

The next morning when the Otis family met at breakfast, they discussed the ghost at some length. The United States Minister was naturally a little annoyed to find that his present had not been accepted.

'I have no wish,' he said, 'to do the ghost any personal injury[9], and I must say that, considering the length of time he has been in the house, I don't think it is at all polite to throw pillows at him' – a very fair remark, at which the twins burst into[10] shouts of laughter. 'On the other hand,' he continued, 'if he really refuses to use the Rising Sun Lubricator, we shall have to take his chains from him. It will be quite impossible to sleep, with such a noise going on outside the bedrooms.'

For the rest of that week, however, they were undisturbed; the only thing that attracted any attention being the continual renewal[11] of the blood-stain on the library floor. This certainly was very strange, as the door was always locked nightly by Mr Otis, and the windows kept closely barred[12].

---

1 hysterics [hɪsˈtɛrɪks] (n.) 歇斯底里發作
2 grin [grɪn] (v.) 露齒而笑
3 spare [spɛr] (a.) 空房間的
4 confine [kənˈfaɪn] (v.) 侷限
5 choke [tʃok] (v.) 窒息
6 drown [draʊn] (v.) 淹死
7 wretched [ˈrɛtʃɪd] (a.) 惱人的
8 revenge [rɪˈvɛndʒ] (n.) 報仇
9 injury [ˈɪndʒərɪ] (n.) 受傷
10 burst into 情緒的突然發作
11 renewal [rɪˈnjuəl] (n.) 更新；復原
12 bar [bɑr] (v.) 閂住

The changing color of the stain also led to a lot of comment. Some mornings it was a dull red, then it would be vermilion[1], then a rich purple, and once when they came down for family prayers they found it a bright emerald-green.

These kaleidoscopic changes naturally amused the family very much, and they made bets[2] on the subject each evening. The only person who did not enter into the joke was little Virginia, who, for some unexplained reason, was always rather upset at the sight of the blood-stain, and very nearly cried the morning it was emerald-green.

The second appearance of the ghost was on Sunday night. Shortly after they had gone to bed they were suddenly frightened by a terrible crash in the hall. Rushing downstairs, they found that a large suit of armor[3] had become detached from its stand[4], and had fallen on the stone floor, while, seated in a high-backed chair, was the Canterville ghost, rubbing his knees with an expression of acute agony on his face.

The twins, who had brought their peashooters[5] with them, at once discharged[6] two pellets[7] at him, with that accuracy of aim[8] which can only be got by long and careful practice on a teacher.

The United States' Minister pointed his pistol at him, and called to him, in accordance with Californian etiquette[9], to hold up his hands! The ghost stared up with a wild shriek[10] of rage, and rushed through them like a mist, putting out Washington Otis's candle as he passed, and so leaving them all in total darkness.

---

1 vermilion [vəˈmɪljən] (a.) 朱紅色的
2 make bets 打賭
3 suit of armor 一整套盔甲
4 stand [stænd] (n.) 置物台；器具架
5 peashooter [ˈpiˌʃutɚ] (n.) 射豆槍玩具
6 discharge [dɪsˈtʃɑrdʒ] (v.) 發射

Frustration

- Why does the Canterville Ghost feel so angry and frustrated?
- Think of a time when you felt frustrated.
- What caused it? What did you do?

On reaching the top of the stairs he recovered himself, and decided to give his famous demon's laughter. This he had on more than one occasion found extremely useful. It was said to have turned Lord Raker's hair grey in a single night, and had certainly made three of Lady Canterville's French governesses[11] leave before their month was up[12]. He accordingly laughed his most horrible laugh, till the old roof rang[13] and rang again, but hardly had the terrible echo died away when a door opened, and Mrs Otis came out in a light blue dressing-gown.

'I am afraid you are far from well,' she said, 'and so I have brought you a bottle of Dr Dobell's medicine. If it is indigestion, you will find it an excellent remedy.'

The ghost looked at her in fury, and began at once to make preparations for turning himself into a large black dog, an accomplishment[14] for which he was justly famous, and to which the family doctor had always attributed the permanent madness of Lord Canterville's uncle.

---

7 pellet [ˈpɛlɪt] (n.) 顆粒狀物；彈丸
8 aim [em] (n.) 瞄準
9 etiquette [ˈɛtɪkɛt] (n.) 禮節
10 shriek [ʃrik] (n.) 尖叫聲
11 governess [ˈɡʌvənɪs] (n.) 家庭女教師
12 up [ʌp] (a.) 結束的
13 ring [rɪŋ] (v.) 迴響
14 accomplishment [əˈkʌmplɪʃmənt] (n.) 成就

The sound of approaching footsteps, however, made him hesitate, so he contented himself with becoming faintly phosphorescent[1], and vanished with a deep churchyard groan, just as the twins had come up to him.

On reaching his room he entirely broke down[2], and became very upset. The vulgarity of the twins, and the materialism of Mrs Otis, were naturally extremely annoying, but what really upset him most was that he had been unable to wear the suit of armor. He had hoped that even modern Americans would be thrilled by the sight of a ghost in armor. Besides, it was his own suit. He had worn it with success at the Kenilworth tournament, and had been highly complimented on it by no less a person than Queen Elizabeth herself. Yet when he had put it on, he had been completely overpowered[3] by its weight, and had fallen heavily on the stone pavement, hurting both his knees seriously, and bruising his right hand.

For some days after this he was extremely ill, and hardly moved from his room at all, except to keep the blood-stain in good condition. However, by taking great care of himself, he recovered, and decided to make a third attempt to frighten the United States Minister and his family.

---

1 phosphorescent [ˌfɑsfəˈrɛsənt] (a.) 發出磷光的
2 break down 崩潰
3 overpower [ˌovəˈpauə] (v.) 壓倒；無法承受

He selected Friday 17th August for his appearance, and spent most of that day looking through his costumes, finally choosing a large hat with a red feather, a shroud[1], and a rusty dagger[2]. Towards evening a violent rainstorm started, and the wind was so strong that all the windows and doors in the old house shook and rattled[3]. In fact, it was just the sort of weather he loved. His plan of action was to go quietly to Washington Otis's room, sit at the foot[4] of the bed, and stab[5] himself three times in the throat to the sound of slow music.

He especially disliked Washington, because he knew that it was he who was in the habit of removing the famous Canterville blood-stain by means of Pinkerton's Paragon Detergent. Having caused a state of total terror in the young man, he was then to move on to the room occupied by the United States Minster and his wife, and there place a cold, damp[6] hand on Mrs Otis's forehead, while he whispered the awful secrets of the mortuary[7] into her trembling husband's ear.

With regard to little Virginia, he had not quite made up his mind. She had never insulted him in any way and was pretty and gentle. A few low groans from the wardrobe, he thought, would be more than sufficient, or, if that failed to wake her, he would pull at her bedcovers with twitching[8] fingers.

---

1 shroud [ʃraʊd] (n.) 裹屍布
2 dagger [ˈdægɚ] (n.) 匕首
3 rattle [ˈrætl̩] (v.) 發出咯咯聲
4 foot [fʊt] (n.) 底部
5 stab [stæb] (v.) 刺
6 damp [dæmp] (a.) 潮濕的

As for the twins, he was quite determined to teach them a lesson. The first thing to do was, of course, to sit on their chests, so as to reproduce the sensation of a nightmare. Then, as their beds were quite close to each other, to stand between them in the form of a green, icy-cold corpse[9] until they became paralyzed with fear, and finally, to throw off the shroud, and crawl[10] around the room, with white bleached[11] bones and one rolling eyeball[12].

Revenge

- What do you think of the ghost's plans for revenge?
- Have you ever decided to "teach someone a lesson"?
- Why? What happened?

At half past ten he heard the family going to bed. For some time he was disturbed by wild shrieks of laughter from the twins, who, with the energy of schoolboys, were evidently amusing themselves before they went to sleep; but at a quarter past eleven all was quiet, and, as midnight sounded, he set off.

7 mortuary [ˈmɔrtʃuˌɛrɪ] (n.) 停屍間
8 twitching [ˈtwɪtʃɪŋ] (a.) 抽搐的
9 corpse [kɔrps] (n.) 屍體
10 crawl [krɔl] (v.) 緩慢移動
11 bleached [blitʃt] (a.) 變白的
12 eyeball [ˈaɪˌbɔl] (n.) 眼珠

The Otis family slept, unconscious of their doom[1], and high above the rain and storm he could hear the steady snoring[2] of the Minister for the United States. He stepped quietly out of the wall, with an evil smile on his cruel, wrinkled[3] mouth. On and on he went, like an evil shadow, the very darkness seeming to hate him as he passed.

He muttered[4] strange sixteenth-century curses[5] as he went, and held up the rusty dagger in the midnight air. Finally he reached the corner of the passage that led to Washington's room. For a moment he paused there, then the clock struck the quarter, and he felt the time had come. He chuckled[6] to himself, and turned the corner. But as soon as he had he done this, he fell back in terror, and hid his white face in his long, bony hands.

Right in front of him was standing a horrible specter[7], still as a sculpture, and as dreadful as a madman's dream! Its head was bald[8] and shiny; its face round, fat and white; and hideous[9] laughter seemed to have changed its features into an eternal grin. Rays of scarlet[10] light shone from its eyes, the mouth was a wide well[11] of fire, and horrible white clothes, like his own, were wrapped around the enormous form. On its chest was a large card with strange antique writing, and with its right hand it held up a magnificent sword.

1 doom [dum] (n.) 厄運
2 snoring ['snorɪŋ] (n.) 打鼾
3 wrinkled ['rɪŋkld] (a.) 起皺紋的
4 mutter ['mʌtɚ] (v.) 低聲含糊地說
5 curse [kɝs] (n.) 咒罵
6 chuckle ['tʃʌkl] (v.) 暗自發笑
7 specter ['spɛktɚ] (n.) 幽靈
8 bald [bɔld] (a.) 禿頭的
9 hideous ['hɪdɪəs] (a.) 可怕的
10 scarlet ['skɑrlɪt] (a.) 鮮紅色的
11 well [wɛl] (n.) 井

Because he hadn't seen a ghost before, he was, naturally, terribly frightened, and after a second quick look at the awful phantom, he ran back to his room. When he was in the privacy of his own apartment, he threw himself down on a small bed and hid his face under the clothes. After a time, however, the brave old Canterville spirit asserted itself[1], and he decided to go and speak to the other ghost as soon as it was daylight.

So, just as the dawn was touching the hills with silver light, he returned towards the spot where he had first seen the terrible phantom, feeling that, after all, two ghosts were better than one, and that, with the help of his new friend, he might safely fight against the twins. On reaching the spot, however, a terrible sight met his eyes.

Something had evidently happened to the specter, for the light had entirely faded[2] from its hollow eyes, the magnificent sword had fallen from its hand, and it was leaning[3] up against the wall in an uncomfortable way.

He rushed forward and seized[4] it in his arms, when, to his horror, the head fell off and rolled onto the floor. He suddenly found himself holding a body made from a white curtain, with a sweeping brush, a kitchen knife and a hollow[5] pumpkin lying at his feet! Unable to understand this strange change, he looked at the card, and there in the grey morning light he read these fearful words:

---

1 assert oneself 顯示自己的權
   威；堅持自己的權利
2 fade [fed] (v.) 光變暗淡
3 lean [lin] (v.) 傾身；倚；靠

4 seize [siz] (v.) 抓住；奪取
5 hollow [ˋhɑlo] (a.) 中空的
6 fake [fek] (n.) 冒牌貨
7 foiled [fɔɪld] (a.) 受挫的

THE OTIS GHOST
The only true and original spook.
Beware of imitations.
All others are fakes.[6]

The whole thing became clear. He had been tricked, foiled[7] and outwitted[8]! The old Canterville look came into his eyes; he raised his withered[9] hands high above his head, and swore that when the cockerel[10] had crowed[11] twice, acts of blood would be done, and Murder would walk about with silent feet.

As soon as he had finished saying this a cock crowed in the distance. He laughed a long, low, bitter laugh, and waited. Hour after hour he waited, but the cock, for some strange reason, did not crow a second time.

---

8 outwitted [aut`wɪtɪd] (a.) 被唬弄的
9 withered [`wɪðəd] (a.) 乾癟的
10 cockerel [`kɑkərəl] (n.) 小公雞

11 crow [kro] (v.) (公雞) 啼叫
（註：《聖經》記載，彼得在雞
啼兩次之前曾三度不認主）

So finally, at half past seven, the arrival of the servants made him give up his wait, and he walked back to his room thinking of his destroyed hopes. There he read several old books, and found that on every occasion he had used this oath[1], the cock had crowed twice.

He then got into a comfortable lead[2] coffin, and stayed there until evening.

The Ghost's Promise

- What does the ghost decide to do when he realizes he has been tricked?
- Why doesn't he do anything in the end?

IV

  The next day the ghost was very weak and tired. The terrible excitement of the last four weeks was beginning to have its effect . For five days he stayed in his room, and at last he decided to give up on the blood-stain on the library floor. If the Otis family did not want it, they clearly didn't deserve it. They were evidently people on a low, material level of existence, and completely incapable of appreciating the symbolic value of serious phenomena.

It was his solemn duty to appear in the corridor once a week and make horrible noises from the large window on the first and third Wednesday of every month, and he didn't see how he could honorably escape from his obligations. It was true that his life had been very evil, but, on the other hand, as a ghost he was very conscientious in all things connected with the supernatural.

1　oath [oθ] (n.) 誓約
2　lead [lɛd] (a.) 鉛製的
3　effect [ɪˋfɛkt] (n.) 作用；影響
4　give up on　忘掉
5　deserve [dɪˋzɝv] (v.) 應得
6　conscientious [ˌkɑnʃɪˋɛnʃəs] (a.) 盡責的

So, for the next three Saturdays he walked along the corridor as usual between midnight and three o'clock, taking every possible precaution against being either heard or seen. He removed his boots, stepped as lightly as possible on the old wooden floor, wore a long black velvet cloak, and was careful to use Rising Sun Lubricator for oiling his chains. But, in spite of[1] everything, he was still attacked.

The twins continually stretched strings[2] across the corridor, which he fell over in the dark. On one occasion he had a severe fall because of a butter slide[3] which they had made at the top of the stairs. This last insult so enraged him, that he decided to assert his dignity, and planned to visit the boys the next night in his celebrated character of the Headless Earl[4].

He had not appeared in this disguise for more than seventy years; it took him three full hours to make his preparations. At last everything was ready, and he was very pleased with his appearance.

At a quarter past one he glided[5] out of the wall and crept[6] down the corridor. On reaching the room occupied by the twins he found the door slightly open. Wishing to make an effective entrance, he pushed it wide open, when a heavy jug[7] of water fell right down on him, wetting him to the skin, and just missing his left shoulder by a couple of inches. At the same moment he heard shrieks of laughter coming from the boys' beds.

---

1 in spite of 儘管
2 string [strɪŋ] (n.) 細繩
3 butter slide 在地板上抹奶油讓人滑倒
4 earl [ɝl] (n.) 伯爵

5 glide [glaɪd] (v.) 滑行
6 creep [krip] (v.) 躡手躡足地走
7 jug [dʒʌg] (n.) 壺

The shock was so great that he ran back to his room as fast as he could go, and the next day he was in bed with a severe cold. The only thing that made him feel a little better was the fact that he hadn't taken his head with him. If he had done, the consequences would have been very serious.

He now gave up all hope of ever frightening this rude American family, and contented himself with creeping about the passages in slippers, with a thick red scarf round his throat for fear of draughts[1], and a small gun in case the twins attacked him.

The final blow[2] occurred[3] on 19th September. He had gone downstairs to the great entrance-hall, feeling sure that he would not be attacked there. He was wearing a long shroud, had tied up his jaw[4] with a strip of yellow cloth, and carried a small lantern and a spade[5]. It was about a quarter past two in the morning, and, as far as he could judge, no-one was moving.

As he was walking towards the library, however, to see if there were any traces left of the blood-stain, two figures suddenly leapt out on him from a dark corner and waved their arms wildly above their heads, and shrieked 'BOO!' in his ear.

1 draught [dræft] (n.) 氣流
2 blow [blo] (n.) 打擊；不幸
3 occur [əˈkɝ] (v.) 發生
4 jaw [dʒɔ] (n.) 下巴
5 spade [sped] (n.) 鏟子
6 panic [ˈpænɪk] (n.) 驚慌
7 stove [stov] (n.) 火爐
8 despair [dɪˈspɛr] (n.) 絕望
9 nutshell [ˈnʌtˌʃɛl] (n.) 堅果殼

Seized with panic[6], which, under the circumstances was only natural, he rushed for the staircase, but found Washington Otis waiting for him with the big garden water pump. To escape his enemies, he vanished into the large iron stove[7], which, fortunately for him, was not lit, and had to make his way home through the pipes and chimneys, arriving at his own room in a terrible state of dirt, disorder and despair[8].

After this, he was not seen again on any nocturnal expedition. The twins waited for him on several occasions, and covered the floor of the corridor with nutshells[9] every night to the great annoyance of their parents and the servants, but it was of no use. It was quite evident that his feelings were so hurt that he would not appear. They assumed that the ghost had gone away, and, in fact, Mrs Otis wrote a letter to that effect to Lord Canterville, who, in reply, expressed his great pleasure at the news, and sent his best congratulations to the Minister's wife.

Changes

- How do the ghost's feelings change throughout the story?
- How does this affect what he does?
- What are your feelings about the ghost?

 The Otises, however, were deceived [1], for the ghost was still in the house. But although he was now almost an invalid, he was by no means ready to let matters [2] rest, particularly as he heard there were guests at the Chase.

Among the guests was the young Duke of Cheshire, whose grand-uncle, Lord Francis Stilton, had once bet a hundred pounds with Colonel Carbury that he would play dice [3] with the Canterville ghost. Lord Francis was found the next morning lying on the floor, and he never in his life said anything again except 'Double Sixes'.

The ghost was naturally very anxious to show that he had not lost his influence over the Stiltons. So, he made arrangements for appearing to the Duke, Virginia's young admirer, in his celebrated impersonation [4] of The Vampire Monk. At the last moment, however, his terror of the twins prevented him leaving his room, and the Duke slept in peace and dreamed of Virginia.

---

1 deceive [dɪˋsiv] (v.) 矇騙
2 let matters rest 善罷干休
3 dice [daɪs] (n.) 骰子（單複數同形）
4 impersonation [ɪmˏpɝsṇˋeʃən] (n.) 模仿
5 tear [tɛr] (v.) 撕開；扯破
6 hedge [hɛdʒ] (n.) 樹籬

A few days after this, Virginia and the young Lord went out riding, and she tore her clothes so badly getting through a hedge, that, on her return home, she decided to go up by the back staircase so as not to be seen.

As she was running past the Tapestry Chamber, the door of which happened to be open, she thought she saw someone inside, and thinking it was her mother's maid, who sometimes worked there, she looked in to ask her to mend her clothes. To her immense surprise, however, it was the Canterville ghost himself! He was sitting by the window, watching the gold leaves of the yellow trees fly through the air, and the red leaves dance madly down the long avenue. His head was leaning on his hand, and his whole attitude was one of extreme depression.

Indeed, he looked so sad and ill that little Virginia, whose first idea had been to run away and lock herself in her room, was filled with pity and decided to try and comfort him. So light was her footfall, and so deep his melancholy, that he did not notice her until she spoke to him.

---

7 tapestry [ˈtæpɪstrɪ] (n.) 掛毯
8 mend [mɛnd] (v.) 修補

9 footfall [ˈfʊt͵fɔl] (n.) 腳步;腳步聲
10 melancholy [ˈmɛlən͵kɑlɪ] (n.) 憂愁

'I am sorry for you,' she said, 'but my brothers are going back to school tomorrow, and then, if you behave yourself, no-one will annoy you.'

'It is absurd[1] asking me to behave myself,' he answered, looking round in astonishment[2] at the pretty little girl who had dared to address him, 'quite absurd. I must rattle my chains, and groan through keyholes, and walk about at night, if that is what you mean. It is my only reason for existing.'

'It is no reason for existing, and you know you have been very wicked. Mrs Umney told us, the first day we arrived here, that you had killed your wife.'

'Well, I admit it,' said the ghost, 'but it was a purely family matter and concerned[3] no-one else.'

'It is very wrong to kill anyone,' said Virginia.

'My wife wasn't pretty, never had my clothes properly[4] ironed, and knew nothing about cookery. However, it doesn't matter now, for it is over, and I don't think it was very nice of her brothers to starve me to death[5], though I did kill her.'

'Starve you to death? Oh, Mr Ghost – I mean Sir Simon – are you hungry? I have a sandwich in my case. Would you like it?'

'No, thank you, I never eat anything now; but it is very kind of you, all the same, and you are much nicer than the rest of your horrid, rude, vulgar, dishonest family.'

---

1 absurd [əb'sɜd] (a.) 荒謬的
2 astonishment [ə'stɑnɪʃmənt] (n.) 驚訝
3 concern [kən'sɜn] (v.) 涉及
4 properly ['prɑpəlɪ] (adv.) 恰當地
5 starve me to death 活活把我餓死

'Stop!' cried Virginia, stamping her foot. 'It is you who are rude, and horrid, and vulgar; and as for dishonesty, I know that you stole the paints out of my box to try and restore[1] that silly blood-stain in the library. First you took all my reds, including vermilion, and I couldn't do any more sunsets, then you took the emerald[2] green and the chrome[3] yellow, and finally I had nothing left but indigo[4] and Chinese white, and could only do moonlight scenes, which are always depressing to look at, and not at all easy to paint. I never told on[5] you, though I was very annoyed, and it was really silly, the whole thing. Whoever heard of emerald-green blood?'

'Well, really,' said the ghost, 'what was I to do? It is very difficult to get real blood nowadays, and, as your brother began it all with his Paragon Detergent, I certainly saw no reason why I should not have your paints.'

'Good evening. I will go and ask father to arrange for the twins an extra week's holiday.'

'Please don't go, Miss Virginia,' he cried. 'I am so lonely and so unhappy, and I really don't know what to do. I want to go to sleep and I cannot.'

'That's quite absurd. You only have to go to bed and blow out the candle. It is very difficult sometimes to keep awake, especially at church, but there is no difficulty at all about sleeping. Why even babies know how to do that, and they are not very clever.'

---

1 restore [rɪˋstor] (v.) 恢復
2 emerald [ˋɛmərəld] (a.) 翠綠色的
3 chrome [krom] (n.) 鉻黃
4 indigo [ˋɪn‚dɪgo] (n.) 深紫藍色顏料
5 tell on 告發
6 wonder [ˋwʌndɚ] (n.) 驚異
7 nightingale [ˋnaɪtɪŋ‚gel] (n.) 夜鶯
8 yew [ju] (n.) 紫杉

'I have not slept for three hundred years,' he said sadly, and Virginia's beautiful blue eyes opened in wonder ; 'for three hundred years I have not slept, and I am so tired.'

Virginia grew quite serious, and her lips trembled. She came towards him, and kneeling down at his side, looked up into his old, withered face. 'Poor, poor Ghost,' she murmured; 'have you no place where you can sleep?'

Sleep

- What do you think the Ghost would like to do?

'Far away behind the woods,' he answered, in a low, dreamy voice, 'there is a little garden. There the grass grows long and deep, the nightingale sings all night long, the cold crystal moon looks down and the yew tree spreads out its giant arms over the sleepers.'

Virginia's eyes filled with tears, and she hid her face in her hands.

'You mean the Garden of Death,' she whispered.

'Yes, Death. Death must be so beautiful. To lie in the soft brown earth, with the grasses waving above one's head, and listen to silence. To have no yesterday, and no tomorrow. To forget time, to forgive life, to be at peace. You can help me. You can open the doors of Death's house, for Love is always with you, and Love is stronger than Death is.'

Virginia trembled, and for a few moments there was silence. She felt as if she was in a terrible dream.

Then the Ghost spoke again, and his voice sounded like the sighing[1] of the wind.

'Have you ever read the old prophecy[2] on the library window?'

'Oh, often,' cried the little girl, looking up. 'I know it quite well. It is painted in strange black letters, and it is difficult to read. There are only six lines:

> When a golden girl can win
> Prayer from out the lips of sin[3],
> When the barren[4] almond bears[5],
> And a little child gives away its tears,
> Then shall all the house be still
> And peace come to Canterville.

But I don't know what they mean.'

'They mean,' he said sadly, ' that you must weep[6] for me for my sins, because I have no tears, and pray for my soul, because I have no faith; and then, if you have been sweet, and good, and gentle, the Angel of Death will have mercy[7] on me.'

---

1 sighing [ˈsaɪɪŋ] (n.) 嘆息
2 prophecy [ˈprɑfəsɪ] (n.) 預言
3 sin [sɪn] (n.)（宗教或道德上的）罪
4 barren [ˈbærən] (a.) 不結果實的
5 bear [bɛr] (v.) 開花結果
6 weep [wip] (v.) 哭泣

Virginia made no answer, and the Ghost was in despair as he looked down at her bowed⁸ golden head. Suddenly she stood up, very pale, and with a strange light in her eyes. 'I am not afraid,' she said firmly, 'and I will ask the Angel to have mercy on you.'

He rose from his seat with a low cry of joy, and, taking her hand, bent over with old-fashioned grace and kissed it. His fingers were cold as ice, and his lips burned like fire, but Virginia did not pull away as he led her across the darkening⁹ room.

When they reached the end of the room, he stopped, and muttered some words she could not understand. She opened her eyes, and saw the wall slowly fading away¹⁰ like a mist, and a great black cavern¹¹ in front of her. A bitter¹² cold wind swept round them, and she felt something pulling at her dress.

'Quick, quick,' cried the Ghost, 'or it will be too late,' and in a moment the wall had closed behind them and the Tapestry Chamber was empty.

The Prophecy

- What does the prophecy mean?
- Where do you think Virginia and the ghost go?

---

7 mercy ['mɝsɪ] (n.) 慈悲；仁慈
8 bowed [bod] (a.) 彎如弓的
9 darkening ['dɑrknɪŋ] (a.) 變黑的
10 fade away 消逝
11 carven ['kɑrvən] (n.) 洞穴
12 bitter ['bɪtɚ] (a.) 嚴寒刺骨的

VI

About ten minutes later, the bell rang for tea, and, as Virginia did not come down, Mrs Otis sent up one of the servants to get her. After a little time he returned and said that he could not find Miss Virginia anywhere. As she was in the habit of going out to the garden every evening to get flowers for the dinner-table, Mrs Otis was not at all alarmed[1] at first, but when six o'clock struck, and Virginia did not appear, she became very worried, and sent the boys to look for her, while she herself and Mr Otis searched every room in the house.

At half-past six the boys came back and said that they could find no trace [2] of their sister anywhere. They were all now in the greatest state of excitement, and did not know what to do. Mr Otis told Washington and two of the servants to search the district [3], then he sent telegrams to all the police inspectors in the county, telling them to look out for a little girl. He then ordered his horse to be fetched [4], and, after insisting that his wife and the three boys sit down to dinner, rode off down the Ascot road with a servant.

1 alarmed [əˈlɑrmd] (a.) 受驚的
2 trace [tres] (n.) 蹤跡
3 district [ˈdɪstrɪkt] (n.) 區；轄區
4 fetch [fɛtʃ] (v.) 帶來

He had hardly, however, gone a couple of miles when he heard somebody galloping[1] after him, and, looking round, saw the little Duke of Cheshire coming up on his pony, with his face very red and no hat.

'I'm awfully[2] sorry, Mr Otis,' gasped[3] out the boy, 'but I can't eat any dinner as long as Virginia is lost. Please don't be angry with me. You won't send me back, will you? I can't go! I won't go!'

The Minister could not help smiling at the handsome young man, and was touched[4] by his devotion to Virginia, so leaning down from his horse, he patted[5] him kindly on the shoulders, and said, 'Well, Cecil, if you won't go back, I suppose you must come with me – but I must get you a hat at Ascot.'

'Oh, bother[6] my hat! I want Virginia!' cried the little Duke, laughing, and they galloped on to the railway station. There Mr Otis asked the station-master if anyone answering the description of Virginia had been seen on the platform, but could get no news of her.

The station-master, however, sent a telegram up and down the line[7], and assured him that a strict watch[8] would be kept for her, and, after having bought a hat for the little Duke, Mr Otis rode off to Bexley, a village about four miles away. There they called on[9] the rural[10] policeman, but could get no information from him, and after riding around for a while, they turned their horses' heads homewards, and reached the Chase at about eleven o'clock, dead[11] tired and almost heartbroken.

---

1 gallop [ˈgæləp] (v.) (馬等) 疾馳
2 awfully [ˈɔfulɪ] (adv.) 〔口〕非常地
3 gasp [gæsp] (v.) 上氣不接下氣
4 touched [tʌtʃt] (a.) 受感動的
5 pat [pæt] (v.) 輕拍
6 bother [ˈbɑðɚ] (v.) 才不管……
7 line [laɪn] (n.) 鐵路線
8 strict watch 詳加檢查

They found Washington and the twins waiting for them at the gate-house [12] with lanterns, as the avenue was very dark. Not the slightest [13] trace of Virginia had been discovered. The fish-pond had been dragged [14], and the whole Chase thoroughly searched, but without any result. It was evident that, for that night at least, Virginia was lost to them; and it was in a state of the deepest depression that Mr Otis and the boys walked up to the house, the servant following behind with the two horses and the pony.

In the hall they found a group of frightened servants, and poor Mrs Otis was lying on a sofa in the library. She was almost out of her mind with terror and anxiety, and was having her forehead bathed [15] with eau-de-cologne [16] by the old housekeeper. Mr Otis at once insisted on her having something to eat, and ordered supper for the whole party. It was a melancholy meal, as hardly anyone spoke, and even the twins were worried and quiet, as they were very fond of [17] their sister.

When they had finished, Mr Otis ordered them all to bed, saying nothing more could be done that night, and that he would telegraph in the morning to Scotland Yard for some detectives to be sent down immediately.

---

9 call on 拜訪；請求
10 rural [ˈrʊrəl] (a.) 鄉間的
11 dead [dɛd] (adv.) 〔口〕極為
12 gate-house [ˈgetˌhaʊs] (n.) 門房
13 slight [slaɪt] (a.) 微小的

14 drag [dræg] (v.) 打撈
15 bathed [bæðd] (a.) 濕透的
16 eau-de-cologne [ˌodəkəˈlon] (n.) 古龍水
17 be fond of 喜歡

Virginia

- Where do you think Virginia is?
- Have you ever 'disappeared'?
- How did people react?

 Just as they were passing out of the dining-room, midnight began to strike from the clock tower, and when the last stroke sounded they heard a crash and a sudden shrill[1] cry and a dreadful clap[2] of thunder shook the house. Some notes of unearthly[3] music floated through the air, a panel at the top of the staircase opened with a loud noise, and Virginia stepped out onto the landing[4], looking very pale and white, with a little casket[5] in her hand.

In a moment they had all rushed up to her. Mrs Otis held her passionately in her arms, the Duke covered her with violent kisses, and the twins did a wild dance round the group.

'Good heavens! child, where have you been?' said Mr Otis, rather angrily, thinking that she had been playing some foolish trick on them. 'Cecil and I have been riding all over the country looking for you, and your mother has been frightened to death. You must never play these practical jokes[6] any more.'

'Except on the Ghost! Except on the Ghost!' shrieked the twins as they danced about.

---

1 shrill [ʃrɪl] (a.) 尖聲的；刺耳的
2 clap [klæp] (n.) 霹靂聲
3 unearthly [ʌnˋɜθlɪ] (a.) 神祕的；鬼怪的
4 landing [ˋlændɪŋ] (n.) 樓梯的平臺
5 casket [ˋkæskɪt] (n.) 小匣（如珠寶匣）
6 practical joke 惡作劇

'My own darling, thank God we have found you; you must never leave my side again,' murmured Mrs Otis, as she kissed the trembling child, and smoothed the tangled gold of her hair.

'Father,' said Virginia quietly, 'I have been with the ghost. He is dead, and you must come and see him. He had been very wicked, but he was really sorry for all he had done, and he gave me this box of beautiful jewels before he died.'

The whole family gazed at her in silent amazement, but she was quite serious; and, turning round, she led them through the opening in the wall down a narrow secret corridor, Washington following with a lighted candle, which he had taken from the table.

Finally, they came to a great oak door. When Virginia touched it, it swung back and they found themselves in a little low room with one tiny window. In the wall was a huge iron ring and chained to it was a skeleton that was stretched out at full length on the stone floor. It seemed to be trying to reach a jug that had once held water, and a plate where there had been food, which were just out of its reach.

Virginia knelt down beside the skeleton, and, folding her hands together, began to pray silently. The rest of the party looked on in wonder at the terrible tragedy whose secret they now understood.

---

7 tangled ['tæŋgld] (a.) 打結的
8 gaze [gez] (v.) 注視
9 swing [swɪŋ] (v.) 擺動
10 out of reach 搆不著

'Hello[1]!' suddenly exclaimed one of the twins, who had been looking out of the window to try and discover in what wing of the house the room was situated. 'Hello! The old almond-tree has blossomed. I can see the flowers quite plainly[2] in the moonlight.'

'God has forgiven him,' said Virginia seriously, as she got to her feet, and a beautiful light seemed to illuminate her face.

'What an angel you are!' cried the young Duke, and he put his arm round her neck and kissed her.

---

1 hello [hə`lo] (int.)（表示驚訝等）嘿；啊
2 plainly [`plenlɪ] (adv.) 清楚地

VII

 Four days after these strange events a funeral[1] started from Canterville Chase at about eleven o'clock at night. The hearse[2] was pulled by eight black horses, and the lead coffin was covered by a rich purple cloth, on which the Canterville coat-of-arms[3] was embroidered[4] in gold. By the side of the hearse walked the servants with lighted torches, and the whole procession was wonderfully impressive.

Lord Canterville was the chief mourner[5], and sat in the first carriage along with Virginia. Then came the United States Minister and his wife, then Washington and the three boys, and in the last carriage was Mrs Umney. They felt that as she had been frightened by the ghost for more than fifty years of her life, she had the right to see the last of him.

They had dug a deep grave[6] in the corner of the churchyard, just under the old yew tree, and the service was read in the most impressive manner by the Rev. Augustus Dampier. When the ceremony[7] was over, the servants, according to an old custom kept by the Canterville family, extinguished[8] their torches, and, as the coffin was being lowered into the grave, Virginia stepped forward and laid on it a large cross made out of white and pink almond blossoms.

As she did so, the moon came out from behind a cloud, and flooded[9] the little churchyard with its silent silver, and from a distant wood a nightingale began to sing. She thought of the ghost's description of the Garden of Death, her eyes filled with tears, and she hardly spoke a word during the drive home.

The Funeral

- How does Virginia feel at the funeral?
- What is the atmosphere like?
- How does the atmosphere change throughout the book?

The next morning, before Lord Canterville went back to London, Mr Otis had a meeting with him on the subject of the jewels the ghost had given to Virginia. They were perfectly magnificent, especially a certain ruby[10] necklace with an old Venetian[11] setting. The jewels were a superb[12] example of sixteenth-century work, and their value was so great that Mr Otis was unsure about allowing his daughter to keep them.

---

1 funeral [`fjunərəl] (n.) 葬禮
2 hearse [hɜs] (n.) 靈車
3 coat-of-arms 盾形章
4 embroider [ɪm`brɔɪdɚ] (v.) 繡上
5 mourner [`mornɚ] (n.) 送葬者
6 grave [grev] (n.) 墓穴

7 ceremony [`sɛrə,monɪ] (n.) 典禮；儀式
8 extinguish [ɪk`stɪŋgwɪʃ] (v.) 熄滅；撲滅
9 flood [flʌd] (v.) 充滿
10 ruby [`rubɪ] (n.) 紅寶石
11 Venetian [və`niʃən] (a.) 威尼斯的
12 superb [su`pɝb] (a.) 一流的

'My Lord,' he said, 'I know the laws of this country and it is quite clear to me that these jewels are, or should be, heirlooms[1] in your family. I would therefore ask you to take them to London with you, and to regard[2] them simply as a part of your property[3] which has been restored to you under strange conditions. As for my daughter, she is only a child, and doesn't yet have, I am glad to say, much interest in such things. Mrs Otis has also told me that these jewels are very valuable and if offered for sale would fetch[4] a very good price. Under these circumstances, Lord Canterville, I feel sure that you will understand how impossible it would be for me to allow them to remain in the possession of any member of my family. Perhaps I should mention that Virginia is very anxious that you should allow her to keep the box as a memento[5] of your unfortunate but misguided[6] ancestor. As it is extremely old, and consequently not in a very good state, you may perhaps be able to agree to her request.'

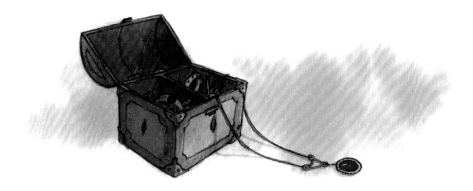

Lord Canterville listened very carefully to the worthy Minister's words, and when Mr Otis had ended, he shook him cordially by the hand, and said, 'My dear sir, your charming little daughter did a great service to my unlucky ancestor. Sir Simon, and I and my family are indebted to her for her marvelous courage. The jewels are clearly hers, and I believe that if I were heartless enough to take them from her, the wicked old fellow would be out of his grave in a fortnight, making my life a misery. As for them being heirlooms, nothing is an heirloom that is not mentioned in a will or legal document, and the existence of these jewels has been quite unknown. I assure you I have no more claim on them than your servants, and when Miss Virginia grows up I am sure she will be pleased to have pretty things to wear, Besides, you forget, Mr Otis, you bought the furniture and the ghost when you bought Canterville Chase, and anything that belonged to the ghost passed at once into your possession.'

The Jewels

- Do you think Mr Otis was right to offer the jewels to Lord Canterville? Why/why not?
- Why did Lord Canterville refuse them?

1 heirloom [ˈɛr‚lum] (n.) 傳家寶
2 regard [rɪˈgɑrd] (v.) 看作
3 property [ˈprɑpɚtɪ] (n.) 財產
4 fetch [fɛtʃ] (v.) 賣得
5 memento [mɪˈmɛnto] (n.) 紀念物
6 misguided [mɪsˈgaɪdɪd] (a.) 誤入歧途的
7 worthy [ˈwɝðɪ] (a.) 可尊敬的
8 cordially [ˈkɔrdʒəlɪ] (adv.) 誠摯地
9 service [ˈsɝvɪs] (n.) 服務；幫助
10 indebted [ɪnˈdɛtɪd] (a.) 受惠的；感激的
11 fortnight [ˈfɔrt‚naɪt] (n.) 十四天；兩星期
12 will [wɪl] (n.) 遺囑
13 claim [klem] (n.) 要求

Mr Otis was distressed[1] at Lord Canterville's refusal, and asked him to reconsider his decision. But he was quite firm[2], and finally convinced the Minister to allow his daughter to keep the present the ghost had given her. When, in the spring of 1890, the young Duchess of Cheshire was presented to the Queen on the occasion of her marriage, her jewels were the universal[3] topic of admiration. For Virginia was married to her fiancé[4] as soon as he came of age[5]. They were both so charming, and they loved each other so much, that everyone was delighted by the marriage.

After the honeymoon[6] was over, the Duke and Duchess went down to Canterville Chase. On the day after they arrived they walked over in the afternoon to the lonely churchyard by the pinewoods. There had been a great deal of difficulty at first about the inscription[7] for Sir Simon's tombstone[8], but finally they decided to engrave[9] it simply with the initials of the old gentleman's name, and the verse from the library window. The Duchess had brought with her some lovely roses, which she put on the grave, and after they had stood by it for some time they walked into the ruined old abbey.

Suddenly, the Duke took hold of her hand and said to her, 'Virginia, a wife should have no secrets from her husband.'

'Dear Cecil! I have no secrets from you.'

'Yes, you have,' he answered, smiling, 'you have never told me what happened to you when you were locked up with the ghost,'

'I have never told anyone, Cecil,' said Virginia seriously.

'I know that, but you might tell me.'

'Please don't ask me, Cecil. I cannot tell you. Poor Sir Simon! I owe him a great deal. Yes, don't laugh, Cecil. I really do. He made me see what Life is, and what Death signifies[10], and why Love is stronger than both.'

Virginia's Secret

- Why do you think Virginia wants to keep her time with the ghost a secret?
- What do you think happened when she went off with the Ghost?
- What things do you keep secret?

1 distressed [dɪ'strɛst] (a.) 痛苦的
2 firm [fɝm] (a.) 堅定的
3 universal [ˌjunə'vɝsl̩] (a.) 普遍的
4 fiancé [ˌfiɑn'se] (n.)〔法〕未婚夫
5 come of age 達到法定年齡

6 honeymoon ['hʌnɪˌmun] (n.) 蜜月假期
7 inscription [ɪn'skrɪpʃən] (n.) 碑文
8 tombstone ['tumˌston] (n.) 墓碑
9 engrave [ɪn'grev] (v.) 刻
10 signify ['sɪgnəˌfaɪ] (v.) 表示

The Duke stood up and kissed his wife lovingly.

'You can have your secret as long as I have your heart,' he murmured.

'You have always had that, Cecil.'

'And you will tell our children some day, won't you?'

Virginia blushed[1].

1 blush [blʌʃ] (v.) 臉紅

AFTER READING

Ⓐ Personal Response

1 What did you think of the story? Did you find it interesting and exciting or boring and predictable? Write a paragraph describing your reaction to the story.

2 Write a 150-word summary of the story.

3 Which character did you like best, and which least? Why?

4 Which of the ghost's appearances would have frightened you most if you'd been at Canterville Chase? Share with a partner.

5 'The Canterville Ghost is not a typical ghost story.' Write a composition discussing this statement.

ⓑ Comprehension

6 Complete this table describing the ghost's five meetings with the Otis family and the reactions of the family members each time.

The Canterville Ghost	The Otis Family's Reactions
ⓐ An old man with clanking chains	① Mr Otis offers him some Tammany Rising Sun Lubricator. ② The twins
ⓑ	① Mr Otis ② The twins ③ Mrs Otis
ⓒ	① The twins
ⓓ	① The twins
ⓔ	① The twins ② Washington

7 Read the poem in the stained-glass window in the library (page 46), and explain in your own words how it refers to Virginia and Sir Simon de Canterville.

8 '*The Canterville Ghost* is a humorous story.' Find examples of comedy in the story.

9 At the start of the story Mrs Umney says that Sir Simon de Canterville "disappeared suddenly in very mysterious circumstances. His body has never been discovered." What do we find out about his death?

10 Mr Otis doesn't want Virginia to have Sir Simon's jewels, and Lord Canterville does. Explain their reasons. What happens in the end? When does she wear them?

11 The ghost uses 'the Fourth Dimension of Space' as a way of escaping from the twins. If space is the fourth dimension, what are the other three dimensions?

12 The author uses three other synonyms for the word ghost. What are they? Do you know any other synonyms? Make a list.

13 Look at these phrases describing things to do with the ghost:

ghastly green light   deep churchyard groan
demon's laughter   green ice-cold corpse
withered hands   cruel, wrinkled mouth

What is the effect of the underlined adjectives, and how are they connected?

14 In Chapter 3 Sir Simon meets the 'Otis Ghost'. How does he react, and what is the irony of his reaction?

15 'The story has a happy ending for everyone.' Explain why this is true.

16 What did the ghost teach Virginia about life and death?

C Characters

17 List the English characters who appear in the book, and say who they are.

18 Complete the table describing the Otis family.

The Otis Family	Appearance and character
Hiram B.	

19 How does Wilde use the following things to show his view of Americans?

- [a] Pinkerton's Champion Stain Remover and Paragon Detergent
- [b] Tammany Rising Sun Lubricator
- [c] Dr Dobell's medicine

20 Who says these things, or who do they refer to? And what do they show about the relationship between the British and the Americans?

- [a] "I come from a modern country, where we have everything money can buy… I reckon that if there were such a thing as a ghost in Europe, we'd have it at home in a very short time in one of our public museums, or on the road as a show."

b) Indeed, in many ways, she was quite English, and was an excellent example of the fact that we really have everything in common with America nowadays, except, of course, language.

c) "I guess the old country is so overpopulated that they don't have enough decent weather for everybody."

21 What do the underlined words tell you about the Canterville Ghost and how is he different from traditional ghosts in other stories?

a) the Canterville ghost stood quite motionless in <u>natural indignation</u>

b) had he been so <u>badly insulted</u>

c) he decided to <u>have revenge</u>

d) with the <u>enthusiasm of true artist</u>, he went over his most <u>celebrated performances</u>

e) he <u>entirely broke down</u>, and became very upset

f) he was, naturally, <u>terribly frightened</u>

g) 'I am so <u>lonely</u> and so <u>unhappy</u>'.

22 Sir Simon has a serious sense of his duties as a ghost. Find quotations which show this attitude, and explain why he feels annoyed with the Otis family.

23 Which characters in the story do you like most, and least, and why? Tell a partner.

24 Imagine you are Mrs Umney. Describe what happens in the house after the Otis family arrives.

25 What questions would ask the ghost? Ask and answer in pairs.

❶ Plot and theme

26 Who is the narrator in 'The Canterville Ghost'?
What effect does this have on the story?

27 What style of plot does the story have? Tick below.

- [a] Flashback (i.e. the story is built up by a narrator looking back at events in the past while living in the present)
- [b] Linear (i.e. a direct movement from beginning to end)
- [c] Cyclical (i.e. it moves around a central event, always returning to that point).

28 Do you think the choice of plot works well?
Why/why not?

29 How would a different ending change the way the story is told?

30 'Wilde takes every opportunity to describe things sensuously.' Find quotations from the story to back this up.

31 What do you suppose happens when Virginia is alone with the ghost? Imagine you are Virginia and write a diary entry describing what happened.

32 Put the events that happened during Virginia's disappearance in the correct order.

_____ a Mr Otis and the Duke rode back to Canterville Chase by 11 o'clock.

_____ b The twins searched the garden and Mr and Mrs Otis searched the house.

_____ c Mr Otis and the Duke rode to the railway station.

_____ d Mr Otis told Washington and 2 servants to search the district.

_____ e Mr Otis and the Duke rode to the village of Bexley.

_____ f The tea bell rang, but Virginia didn't appear.

_____ g Mr Otis ordered everyone to bed.

_____ h Mrs Otis and the twins and the Duke sat down to dinner.

_____ i The whole family sat down for a melancholy supper.

_____ j The Duke rode after Mr Otis on his pony.

33 How does Wilde keep up the excitement of the hunt for Virginia?

34 'The Canterville Ghost is a story of Good triumphing over Evil.' Write a composition to explain this statement, and illustrate your points with suitable quotations.

35 Do you think that the humor took away from the serious points being made in the story? Give reasons why/why not.

TRANSLATION

作者簡介　奧斯卡・王爾德，1854 年生於都柏林，父親是一位出色的外科醫師，母親是一位詩人和作家。他在都柏林攻讀古典文學之後，轉往就讀於牛津大學的莫德林學院，期間曾獲得一個詩的獎項，開始擁有許多的詩迷。1881 年，他出版了第一本著作《詩集》。1884 年，他和康絲坦絲・勞德結婚。他為兒子們寫了出色的童話故事，後來出版為《快樂王子》，大受歡迎。

王德爾在當了兩年的報社編輯之後，重返文壇，才華也更受肯定了。1890 年，他出版了小說《道林・格雷的畫像》，因為故事主人翁有失道德倫理，所以在維多利亞的社會裡掀起波瀾。

一年之後，他又出版了《亞瑟・沙維爵士的罪行》，這本書的故事《老鬼當家》即收錄其中。隨後的劇本《溫夫人的扇子》（1892 年）、《無足輕重的女人》（1893 年）、《理想的丈夫》（1895 年）和《不可兒戲》（1895 年），讓他獲得名氣。劇中諷刺了維多利亞時代的道德和社會禁忌，揭露虛偽的一面，展露了幽默機智的筆鋒。

然而在 1895 年，王爾德密友——阿弗烈德・道格拉斯——他的父親昆斯貝理侯爵，公開控告王爾德誘拐他的兒子，王爾德反告他毀謗，但侯爵最後勝訴，王爾德因而鋃鐺入獄兩年。

在服刑期間，王爾德寫了《深淵書簡》，這本書在他去世之後才出版，另外寫了一本《瑞丁監獄之歌》（1898 年），描繪不堪的牢獄生活。他出獄之後破產，身心俱病，後來旅居國外。1900 年，卒於巴黎。

本書簡介　《老鬼當家》於 1891 年出版，收錄在《亞瑟・沙維爵士的罪行》的成人故事集裡，內容有六篇新寫的故事，另外還有兩篇作者最受歡迎的兒童故事〈快樂王子〉和〈忠實的朋友〉。本書故事描繪一個美國家庭（歐提斯家），向一位英國貴族（康德維爵士）買下一棟房子後所發生的故事。這棟房子鬧鬼，賽門・康德維爵士的鬼魂在這裡已經有三百年了。這個美國家庭起先不相信有鬼，後來鬼出現之後，他們就捉弄鬼，並沒有被嚇到。這讓鬼魂很挫折，覺得自己很沒有用。最後多虧這個美國家庭的小女兒，在她好心的幫助之下，鬼魂終於得以入土為安。

鬼故事在英國的維多利亞時代很受歡迎，有很多大作家都寫了鬼故事，像是狄更斯（Charles Dickens）、特洛普（Anthony Trollope）和科林斯（William Wilkie Collins），不過王爾德寫的鬼故事是比較創新的，故事中的鬼並不令人害怕，反而比較教人同情。王爾德也在行文中調侃了英國的貴族與傳統，還有美國人的簡單直接，以及膚淺的世界觀和對英國的優越感。這在故事中有諸多趣味的著墨。

這個故事還闡述了王爾德的美學觀。故事中富於視覺印象上的描寫，有許多引人入勝的細節描繪，像是美麗的維琪妮雅感化了鬼魂，就反映了王爾德對美的信仰，認為美可以改善事物。維琪妮雅和柴郡公爵的愛情故事，是維多利亞時代典型的浪漫故事，劇情通俗。然而這個幽默有趣的鬼故事，透過王爾德特有的諷刺筆觸，顯得更令人玩味。

I

P.11

美國公使希倫‧歐提斯先生買下了康德維大莊園的時候，大家都跟他說他太不明智了，因為那個地方百分之百確定在鬧鬼。連為人正派的康德維爵士本人在和他談房子買賣時，都覺得自己有義務要告訴歐提斯先生這件事。

康德維爵士說：「我們自己都不想住在這裡了，因為我姑婆——伯頓公爵夫人——她有一次換衣服準備去用晚餐時，突然有一雙骷髏手搭在她的肩膀上，嚇得她魂飛魄散，到現在都還沒有完全回過魂來。歐提斯先生，我想我有責任要告訴你，我們家族中有幾個還活著的親人都看過這個鬼，連教區的牧師——奧古斯都‧鄧波牧師——也都親眼見過。公爵夫人不幸被嚇壞之後，年紀較輕的僕人都不肯再待在這裡了；走廊和書房也會傳來奇怪的聲音，讓康德維夫人晚上常常失眠。

P.12

公使答道：「爵士，貴府的家具和鬼魂，我都會算進買價裡。敝國乃一現代化國家，金錢可以買得到的東西，一項不缺。我們的年輕人對歐洲趨之若鶩，重金挖走你們頂尖的紅伶和歌伶，我猜如果歐洲真的有鬼魂存在，很快地，就會在敝國的國家博物館裡看到，或是在各地巡迴展出。」

康德維爵士笑了一下說道：「我也不怕我們買賣談不成，我得跟你說，是真的有鬼。這個鬼已經鬧了三百年了，確切地來說，從一五八四年就出現了，只要我們家族有人快要過世，他就會現身。」

「那麼，家庭醫生也會繼之出現，對吧，康德維爵士。但是啊，鬼這種東西根本是子虛烏有的事。」

「既然你不介意家裡頭住了個鬼，那我也就不便多說，但你可得記住我說過的這些話。」康德維爵士說道。

歐提斯先生

- 有哪些原因，讓你覺得歐提斯先生不相信有鬼？
- 你個人相信有鬼的存在嗎？

　　幾個星期之後，這樁買賣完成，公使一家人一路來到康德維莊園。歐提斯夫人閨名露桂夏・達潘，以前住在紐約西五十三街，是紐約的一位名媛。如今步入中年，風韻猶存，有一雙動人的明眸，風姿綽約，而且身強體健，活力充沛。她在很多方面看起來都像個英國人，讓人不得不承認，除了語言，英國人和美國人事實上是同一個樣子的。

　　她的大兒子叫做華盛頓，這是父母在一時興起的愛國心下所取的名字，讓兒子一直感到困擾。兒子有一頭秀髮，長得年輕俊俏，舞跳得很好，在倫敦享有名氣。他唯一的缺點，就是太迷戀梔子花，而且對自己貴族出身的血統有優越感。除此之外，他算是很懂事的。

　　維琪妮雅・歐提斯小姐芳齡十五，她靈巧可愛，一雙大大的藍眼睛，看起來很灑脫。在維琪妮雅的下面還有一對活潑好動的雙胞胎弟弟。

　　康德維莊園離最近的亞斯卡火車站有七英里遠，歐提斯先生打了封電報，囑咐一輛輕馬車來接他們，一家人於是高高興興地坐上馬車出發。

　　時值七月，暮色迷人，空氣中彌漫著松香，不時傳來斑尾鴿的啁啾聲，或是瞧見雉的身影。小松鼠從山毛櫸樹上目送他們一路經過，野兔的白色尾巴往空中一躍，溜進灌木叢裡。

　　然而當馬車轉進康德維莊園的大道時，天空突然烏雲密佈，空氣中一陣奇怪的凝結感，在駛向房子之際，落下了偌大的雨滴。

　　房子前的階梯上站著一位老婦人，等著迎接他們。老婦人一身黑色的絲質衣服，戴著一頂白色的帽子，圍著一條白色的圍裙，穿著很整齊。這是管家溫內太太，她用舊式的口吻說道：「歡迎大駕光臨康德維莊園。」

　　他們跟著溫內太太穿過都鐸風格的大廳，走進書房。書房是一個狹長低矮的房間，四壁貼著黑色橡木，房間那一頭有一大扇彩色玻璃窗。他們看到桌上有為他們備好了的茶，他們於是坐下來，四處打量，溫內太太則在一旁伺候著。

　　忽然，歐提斯夫人看到壁爐前的地板上有一塊暗紅色的污痕，她也沒多想，就對溫內太太說：「我看地板是被什

麼東西濺到了。」

老管家壓低聲音答道：「是的，太太，那個地方被血濺到了。」

P.16

歐提斯夫人叫了起來：「太可怕了！我可不想看到客廳裡有血跡，一定要馬上清掉！」

老管家笑了笑，神祕兮兮地低聲說：「那是伊麗諾·康德維夫人的血，她就是在這裡被她丈夫賽門·康德維爵士所殺的，那一年是一五七二年。九年之後，賽門爵士忽然神祕地失蹤，下落始終不明，但他那罪孽深重的鬼魂一直沒有離開莊園。這塊血跡不能洗掉，光觀客和人群都會慕名而來。」

「真是胡說八道！」華盛頓·歐提斯大聲說道：「用品克冠軍除漬劑和百落清潔劑，就可以立刻把血跡清掉。」被嚇到的老管家還來不及阻止，華盛頓已經跪在地上，用小小一根像黑色眉筆的東西在地上刮著。不一會兒工夫，就看不見血跡了。

「我就知道品克很好用！」他得意地對著家人叫道，家人也一副很佩服的樣子。然而，他話才剛說完，一道強烈的閃電照亮昏暗的房間，接著一陣轟隆的雷聲嚇得大家直跳起來。溫內太太應聲昏倒在地。

「什麼鬼天氣嘛！」美國公使大人一邊點燃長雪茄，一邊慢條斯理地說著：「我看啊，這個古老的國家人口實在太多，沒有夠多的好天氣可以分給每一個人。」

P.17

「親愛的希倫老公，這位女士昏倒了，我們該怎麼辦？」歐提斯夫人大聲說道。

「罰她錢，只要她再昏倒或是打破東西，就罰她錢，這就她就再也不會昏倒了。」公使大人回答。

沒過幾分鐘，溫內太太甦醒過來。這下她可犯愁了，她警告歐提斯先生說，小心房子裡會出事情。

她說：「先生，我是親眼看見過的，連教徒會也被嚇得毛髮直豎。這裡曾發生過的恐怖事情，讓我好幾個夜晚都無法闔眼睡覺！」

面對這位真誠的僕人，歐提斯夫婦好心地保證說他們並不怕鬼。老管家祈求上帝保佑她的新主人，在調整提高了薪水之後，老管家離開走回自己的房間。

氣氛

· 康德維莊園彌漫著什麼樣的氣氛？
· 天氣會影響你的心情嗎？

II

P.18

這個夜晚刮起了狂風驟雨，鬧了一整夜，但沒有什麼特別的事情發生。第二天早上，大家下樓用餐，卻看到地板上又浮現出了那塊可怕的血跡。

「我想這不能怪品克冠軍除漬劑，因

為我以前用都很有效。」華盛頓說：「這一定是鬼魂在作怪。」

說完，他就又把血跡擦掉。但是到了隔天早上，血跡又出現了。

晚上時，歐提斯先生親手將書房上了鎖，還帶著鑰匙上樓，然而第三天早上，情況還是一樣。

於是這一家子的興致又來了，歐提斯先生開始懷疑自己是不是太鐵齒了，不相信這世界上有鬼；歐提斯夫人說她想參加靈異學會。這一晚，他們都相信了世界上有鬼的存在，而且從此深信不移。

這天，天氣溫煦，他們一家人趁著傍晚的涼風，出門兜風，一直到了九點才回家，簡單地用了晚餐。餐桌上，一家人都沒聊到鬼魂的事情，也沒有任何預期會撞鬼的心理準備。

P.19

沒有人提及靈異事件，也沒有人提到賽門‧康德維爵士的名字。到了十一點，一家人準備就寢。十一點半時，房子裡全都熄燈了。一陣子後，歐提斯先生房間外的走廊傳來奇怪的聲音，吵醒了歐提斯先生。這個聲音聽起來像是金屬的鏗鏘聲，而且越來越近。

歐提斯先生立刻從床上爬起來，他

點了根火柴，看了一下時鐘，剛好是凌晨一點。他倒是很冷靜，先摸摸自己的脈搏，確定自己的脈搏很正常。奇怪的聲音繼續傳來，而且還伴隨著清晰的腳步聲。他穿上拖鞋，從抽屜裡拿出一個小玻璃瓶，然後打開房門。

在微弱的月光下，他的眼前出現了一個相貌恐怖的老人。老人的眼睛像燒炭那樣紅，一頭的灰色長髮披在肩上，頭髮粘得一團一團的；他穿著古時候的衣服，又髒又破；他的手腕和腳踝都繫著沉重的鐐銬，鐵鍊都生鏽了。

歐提斯先生說：「先生，您好，您這些鏈子一定要上點油了，所以我為您準備了一小瓶坦慕尼旭日潤滑油，聽說一用就有效。我把這瓶潤滑油放在臥室外的燭臺邊，如果您還有需要，我很樂意再拿幾瓶給您。」

P.21

說完，這位美國公使就把瓶子放在大理石桌上，然後關門走回去睡覺。

這個康德維鬼魂站在那裡發愣了一會兒，不由自主地一陣惱怒，接著使勁地把小瓶子摔在光滑的地板上。他沿著走廊奔去，發出哼哼的聲音，渾身發散出鬼魅的綠光。而就在這時候，當他來

到橡木做的大樓梯口時，一扇門忽然打開，出現兩個小小的身影，接下一個大枕頭就飛過他的頭頂！説時遲那時快，鬼魂匆匆利用第四空間的優勢脱逃，遁入牆中，房子又恢復了寂靜。

鬼魂逃回房子左廂的一間小密室裡，倚著一束月光喘口氣，開始尋思自己的處境。三百年來，在他光輝的鬼魂生涯裡，頭一次這樣慘遭羞辱。

康德維鬼魂

・面對康德維鬼魂，歐提斯先生的反應是什麼？這讓鬼魂作何感想？
・你想，那「兩個小小的身影」是什麼？
・鬼魂是如何逃脱的？

P.22

他想起那位老公爵夫人，她站在鏡子前面穿衣服、戴鑽石時，被他嚇得當場昏厥；還有那四個女僕，他只不過是在一個空房間的窗簾後面對她們露齒笑，她們就被嚇得歇斯底里，四處奔逃；還有，教區牧師那晚從書房走出來時，他只是把燭火吹熄，牧師到現在還是神經兮兮的；還有德崔莫老夫人，一天清晨醒來，看到一具骷髏頭坐在壁爐邊的扶手椅上讀她的日記，就整整臥床六個星期高燒不退。

他記得那個恐怖的夜晚，當時，心術不正的康德維爵士在更衣室被人發現喉嚨裡吞進了半張撲克牌，他在噎死之前，供出了自己打撲克牌時耍老千，詐贏了查爾斯・詹姆士・福克斯五萬英鎊，並發誓説是鬼魂逼他吞下紙牌的。

他回憶自己所有的豐功偉業：一個男管家飲彈自盡，只因為看到有一隻綠色的手在敲著窗戶的玻璃；還有，美麗的史達菲爾夫人，她總要在頸子上繫上一條黑色絲絨帶，以掩飾烙在雪白肌膚上的五個指印，後來還在花園的魚池裡跳水自盡。

鬼魂細數著自己這些鬼才般的傑作，自我陶醉不已。但在這之後，竟來了這些不知天高地厚的現代美國人，居然要送他潤滑油，還對著他的頭扔枕頭！是可忍，孰不可忍！再説，窮究古今，沒有鬼曾受到這種屈辱。他決心展開報復，一直到東方泛白，他還沉緬在思緒之中。

III

P.23

翌日早上，歐提斯一家人聚在一起吃早餐，花了些時間討論了鬼的事情。美國公使發現自己的禮物被糟蹋，有一點兒不高興。

他説：「我無意對這個鬼魂做作任何的人身傷害，而且我得這麼説，念及他好歹在這個房子住了那麼久，我認為向他丟枕頭，有失禮數。」這話説得倒是公允，那對雙胞胎兄弟卻聽得一陣爆笑。公使接著説道：「話説回來，如果他真的不肯用坦慕尼旭日潤滑油，我們就得把他身上的鐵鍊拿下來才行，不然臥室外面這麼吵，是很難好好睡覺的。」

這星期的接下來幾天，平靜無事，唯一會讓人留神的，就是書房地板上的血跡還是不斷地出現。這件事是頗為詭異，因為歐提斯先生每晚都會把書房鎖上，窗戶也都會緊緊拴好。

P.24

還有，血跡的顏色竟會變化，這引起了諸多討論。有幾天早上是暗紅色，然後變成朱紅色，接著又變成深紫色，還有一次，當全家人下樓作禱告時，竟然還變成了翠綠色。

顏色像萬花筒這樣變來變去，自然讓這一家人覺得很有趣。每天晚上，他們都會打賭血跡明天會變成什麼顏色。唯一不感興趣的是維琪妮雅小姐，她一看到血跡，就會莫名地生氣，看到翠綠色血跡的那天早上，還差點哭了出來。

週日夜晚，鬼魂才再度現身。全家上床睡覺後不久，大廳傳來了一陣巨響，大家一陣驚嚇。他們紛紛衝到樓下，原來是一副大盔甲從座上掉了下來，倒在石頭地板上，而康德維鬼魂就坐在一張高背椅上揉著膝蓋，露出痛苦萬分的表情。

那對雙胞胎隨身帶了玩具槍下來，不由分說立刻向他射出兩發子彈。從他們的神射度來看，應該是充分練習過如何瞄準老師。

而美國公使拿著手槍指著鬼，並且依照加州的規矩，叫他把手舉起來！鬼魂眼睛往上一瞪狂狂吼大聲尖叫，一陣煙似地穿過他們，在經過華盛頓·歐提斯時，吹熄了他的蠟燭，頓時一片黑暗。

P.25

挫折

· 康德維鬼魂為什麼感到這麼生氣和挫折？
· 回憶一下你自己的挫折經驗。
· 你當時為什麼感到挫折？你當時是如何處理的？

鬼魂來到樓頂時才冷靜下來，決定使出他著名的鬼哭神號的招式。這招很管用，他用過好幾次。據說這招曾讓雷克大人的頭髮一夜變白，而且半途嚇跑過康德維夫人的三個法國女教師。於是他發出最恐怖的笑聲，在老舊的屋頂間響徹不斷，直到歐提斯夫人睡著淺藍色的睡袍，打開房門走出來，淒厲的回音才戛然而止。

「我看啊，你是身體欠安，所以帶了一瓶杜背大夫的藥要給你。這種藥對消化不良尤其有效。」

鬼魂聽得氣炸了，兩眼直瞪著她，正準備要變成一隻大黑狗。這也是他非常有名的一招。康德維爵士的舅舅得了失心瘋，家庭醫生一直都把病因歸咎於這一招。

P.26

而就在這時候，鬼魂忽然聽到有腳步聲接近。他遲疑了一下，最後化為淡淡的磷光，發出一聲陰森林的低吟聲，在雙胞胎趕到之前消失無蹤。

鬼魂回到自己的房間之後，整個崩潰了，悲惱不已。雙胞胎那麼粗野，歐提斯夫人那麼拜物，這固然讓他很生

實在說是最對他的味了！他的行動計畫是這樣的：先悄悄溜進華盛頓・歐提斯的房間去，坐在床腳邊，然後舉起匕首，用慢板的節奏速度，往自己的喉嚨戳三次。

他是對華盛頓特別不滿的，因為就是他每天用品克冠軍除漬劑，把馳名的康德維血跡擦掉的。等到把這個年輕人搞瘋之後，接下來就是去美國公使夫婦的房間，一方面把他那又冰又濕的手，擱在歐提斯夫人的額頭上，另一方面在顫抖不已的歐提斯先生耳邊，嘶嘶地道出這棟屋子裡那間停屍房的駭人祕密。

至於維琴尼亞小姐，他倒還沒想到該怎麼處置。她沒有羞辱過他，而且美麗又溫柔。或許在她的衣櫃裡發出幾聲呻吟就夠了，如果她沒被嚇醒，就再用僵硬的指頭抓抓她的床罩。

P.29

至於那對雙胞胎，他決定一定要好好教訓他們一頓才行。第一步自然就是坐在他們胸口上，製造鬼壓床的效果。然後，既然他們倆的床靠得很近，那他就變成一個慘綠冰冷的屍體，站在他們中間。等到他們嚇得全身發軟，再把裹屍布脫掉，只剩下白骨和一個轉來轉去的眼球，然後在房間裡爬來爬去。

氣，不過最讓他懊惱的，是他無法穿上甲冑。他原本希望這些現代的美國人起碼會被穿著盔甲的鬼嚇到，何況這副盔甲本來就是屬於他的，他還曾經穿著這副盔甲在肯窩比武大會上得勝，伊麗莎白女王本人的親自嘉許。然而，他剛剛想穿上甲冑的時候，無法承受盔甲的重量，害他重重地摔在石板地上，兩個膝蓋摔得好疼，右手也擦傷了。

接下來幾天，他病得很厲害，幾乎無法走出門，能做的只有去把血跡翻新。不過，經過幾天調養，他慢慢地復元了，並且決定第三次出馬，一定要嚇壞美國公使一家人。

P.28

他挑了八月十七日星期五這個日子現身。他花了快一整天的時間挑衣服，最後決定戴一頂有紅羽毛的大帽子，披著裹屍布，配戴一把生銹的匕首。向晚時分，刮起了一場大風雨，疾風震得整個城堡的門窗都嘎嘎作響。這種天氣，

復仇

• 你覺得鬼魂的復仇計畫如何？
• 你曾經想「好好教訓過某人」嗎？
• 為什麼？結果發生了什麼事？

十點半，他聽到一家人紛紛就寢，但那對雙胞胎不時發出尖銳的笑聲，讓他很心煩。顯然，這兩個精力旺盛的男孩在上床前還一直鬧著玩。到了十一點十五分，一切終於沉寂下來。午夜鐘聲一響，他便動身了。

P.30

歐提斯一家人都入睡了，完全沒有想到自己的劫數已到。儘管外頭風大雨大，鬼魂還是聽得到美國公使規律的鼾聲。他悄悄地穿牆而出，乾癟冷酷的嘴上掛著一抹猙獰的微笑。他像個邪惡的影子，一步步飄移前進著，他的來到，彷彿連黑暗都嫌棄。

他一路前進著，口中啐著十六世紀罵人的話，對著黑夜揮著那支生鏽的匕首。最後他來到走廊口，轉過去就是華盛頓的房間了。他在這裡佇立了一會兒，這時十二點一刻鐘響，他覺得時機已到。他咳了一聲，步入走廊，誰知一轉進去，他就嚇得跌坐在地上，把蒼白的臉埋進長長的骷髏手裡。

他的眼前，居然站著一個可怕的鬼，像個雕像一樣動也不動，這簡直是瘋子才會做的可怕惡夢。那個鬼的頭光光禿禿的，他的臉又圓又肥又白，而且笑得很恐怖，五官都扭曲了，好像永遠都會齜牙咧嘴。他的眼睛裡還散發出紅光，嘴巴噴出很大的火焰，而且跟他一樣穿著嚇人的白色衣服，只是身體大了好幾號。在他的胸前還掛著一張大紙卡，上面寫著奇怪的古文，右手還舉著一把亮晶晶的大刀。

P.32

他從來也沒見過其他的鬼，自然是嚇壞了。他又瞄了這個惡鬼一眼，連忙拔腿跑回自己的房間。回到自己隱蔽的房間之後，他倒在小床上，把臉埋進床單裡。過了好一會兒，這個老鬼才重拾了勇氣。他決定，天一亮就去找另一個鬼談。

所以，一等到晨曦爬上山頭，他就走回第一次撞鬼的地點。他想，兩個鬼總強過一個鬼，而且有了新朋友的幫忙，說不定很快就可以順利地把雙胞胎解決掉。但就在他走到現場時，一個恐怖的景象又映入了眼簾。

那個鬼顯然出了什麼岔子，空洞洞的雙眼完全沒有了光芒，手上的大刀也掉了下來，整個身子倚在牆上，非常的古怪。

他連忙上前去，抓住手臂要將之扶起來，但讓他很驚恐的是，頭顱竟掉了下來，還在地板上滾動著。這時，他才突然發現自己抓住的是一個白色窗簾做成的身體，還插著掃帚把，腳邊則是一把廚房菜刀和一個挖空的南瓜！他不明白發生了什麼事，他看著紙卡，在晞微的晨光中讀到下面這些嚇人的字眼：

P.33

這是歐提斯之鬼
這是唯一真正的鬼
小心有人模仿
若有他鬼，皆為仿冒

這下他才整個明白了！他被設計、被坑、被打敗了！他的眼中重新燃起昔日雄風，他把乾癟的手高舉過頭，發誓說，公雞二度高啼之際，必有見血之事發生，殺人事件將默默登場。

他一發誓完，遠處就傳來一聲雞啼。他長笑一聲，聲音低沉而苦澀。他靜待著，時辰一個個過去，但不知怎地，就是聽不到第二次的雞啼。

P.34

最後，七點半了，傭人都起來做事了，他只好放棄，踱回房間，心有未甘。他翻了幾本古書，發現每次只要這樣發誓，公雞都會啼叫第二次的。

之後他就溜進一個很舒適的鉛製棺材裡，靜待夜晚的降臨。

鬼魂的承諾

- 鬼魂發現自己被耍之後，決定做什麼事？
- 鬼魂最後為什麼什麼事都沒做？

P.35

第二天，鬼魂覺得很虛弱、很疲倦。這四個星期以來，飽受驚嚇，讓他開始出現症狀了。他在房間裡足足待了五天，最後，他決定要放棄書房地板上的血跡。既然歐提斯這家人不懂得欣賞，那他們也就不配看到血跡。這些人看來就是屬於低層次的物質存在，完全無法欣賞靈異現象所隱含的價值意義。

每星期在走廊現身一次，每個月的第一個和第三個星期三在大窗戶前面弄些可怕的聲音，是他的重要職責，他是無法規避這些責任而不愧於心的。他生前是罪業盈身的沒錯，但做了鬼之後，他對於裝神弄鬼的事是很盡忠職守的。

P.36

所以接下來的三個週六,他在子夜至凌晨三點之間,會照樣在走廊上來回走動,並且作好各種防護措施,以防被人看到或聽到。他把靴子脫掉,在老舊的木板上盡量輕聲走路,他還會穿上長長的黑絲絨斗篷,並在鐵鍊上仔細地抹上了坦慕尼旭日潤滑油。然而,儘管如此,他還是慘遭攻擊。

雙胞胎兄弟持續在走廊上拉起繩索,讓他在黑暗中絆倒。有一次他還摔得很嚴重,因為他們在第一個階梯塗上了奶油。此舉讓他動了大怒,為了維護自己的尊嚴,他打算隔夜以他著名的「無頭伯爵」這個身分去造訪雙胞胎。

他有七十餘年沒用過這個扮相了,他花了整整三個小時才完成準備工作。最後,所有細節都準備好了,他對自己的樣子感到很滿意。

一點十五分,他穿牆而出,沿著走廊來到雙胞胎的房間外面,發現房門微開。他想製造良好的入場效果,便一把把門推開,未料一大桶水應聲落下,潑了他一身,桶子差一點就砸到他的左肩,應時床上還傳來男孩刺耳的笑聲。

P.38

這次可把鬼魂嚇壞了,他飛快地逃回自己的房間。第二天,他得了重感冒。整件事情唯一值得安慰的是,他沒把自己的頭拎去,要不然後果可能更嚴重。

到了這個時刻,他徹底放棄了,不再奢望能嚇到這個無禮的美國家庭。他只要能夠穿著拖鞋,在走廊偷偷繞個幾圈,他就滿足了。他頸子上還要圍一條紅色圍巾,以防傷風,並隨身帶上一把小槍,以免受到雙胞胎的突擊。

九月十九日,發生了最後一次的打擊。他走下樓,來到寬敞的玄關大廳。他想,在這個地方就不會遇到襲擊了。這時,他穿著長裹屍布,用一塊黃色的布把下巴包起來,拿著一盞小燈籠和一個鏟子。這時,是凌晨兩點一刻,他確信沒有四下都沒有動靜。

就在他往書房移動,想去看看還有沒有血跡留下來的時候,突然從一個暗暗的角落跳出兩個人影,各自舉高雙手在他頭上亂揮一通,還對著他的耳朵尖叫著:「砰!」

P.39

遇到這種情況,他自然是驚惶失措。他往樓梯竄逃,誰知華盛頓·歐提

斯就在那兒等著，還拿著一個很大的花園噴霧器。為了逃出敵人的重圍，他遁入大壁爐，還好壁爐裡沒有升火。接著他順著暖氣管和煙囪，一路溜回自己的房間，這時他已經是灰頭土臉、狼狽不堪，心裡頭失望透頂。

在經過了這件事情之後，就沒見到他在夜裡出沒過。雙胞胎在幾個角落埋伏過，每晚還在走道上撒核桃殼（這弄得父母和下人都頗為不滿），但都撲了空。看來這個鬼魂的自尊心受傷太深，不願再出現了。他們猜想，鬼魂已經離開了，歐提斯夫人甚至還寫了封信給康德維爵士。康德維爵士回信說，聽到這個消息深感欣慰，並祝賀了公使夫人。

改變

- 在故事中，鬼魂的心情有怎樣的改變過程？
- 這如何影響了他的行為？
- 你對這個鬼魂抱以何種心情？

P.40

不過，歐提斯這家人想錯了，鬼魂還住在這棟屋子裡。他一時之間是消聲匿跡了，但他並不打算就此罷休，尤其這時他聽到莊園裡有訪客要來了。

在這一行訪客中，有一位年輕的柴郡公爵，他的舅公法蘭西斯·史提頓曾經和卡柏利上校打賭一百鎊，說要和康德維的鬼魂玩骰子，次日早上卻發現他倒在地板上，從此口裡只會說「雙六」，再也無法說其他的話。

鬼魂自然急於表現自己對史提頓家族的影響力不減，所以他打算以頗受好

評的「吸血鬼修士」扮相，現身給公爵瞧瞧。這位公爵是維琪妮雅的愛慕者。只不過，到了最後關頭，他對於雙胞胎的恐懼感，讓他不敢出房門，所以年輕的公爵得以安睡，夢著他的維琪妮雅。

V

P.41

過了幾天，維琪妮雅和年輕的公爵外出騎馬，結果在穿越樹籬時衣服被勾破了，所以回家後，決定從後方的樓梯上樓，免得被人看見。

當她跑過掛毯室時，門剛好沒有關，她看到有人在裡面。她猜想那可能是母親的侍女，因為她有時會在那裡做活。維琪妮雅便探頭進去，想找她補衣服。結果她嚇了一大跳，裡頭居然是康德維之鬼！鬼魂坐在窗邊，望著枯黃樹上的金色落葉在空中飄落，看著長長的馬路上飛揚的紅色樹葉。他用一隻手撐著頭，全身上下說不出的落寞。

小維琪妮雅本來想轉身就跑，躲回自己的房間，但是看到鬼魂那樣悲傷的病容，頓時升起惻隱之心，想安慰他一下。因為她的腳步很輕，沉緬在憂鬱之中的鬼魂，沒有發現到有人來了，直到她開口說話。

P.42

「我很同情你，我弟弟明天就會回學校了，所以只要你不鬧事，沒有人會來煩你的。」她說。

「叫我別鬧事？豈有此理！」他答道，用訝異的表情，回頭看著這個膽敢和他說話的漂亮小女孩。「豈有此理嘛！我一定要把鐵鍊弄得嘎嘎響，對著鑰匙洞呻吟，在夜裡走來走去，這就是你所謂的鬧事吧。我非得這麼做不行，那是我存在的唯一理由。」

「那才不是什麼存在的理由呢，你也知道你以前做了滔天的惡事。溫內太太跟我們說過了，我們第一天來到這裡時，他就說你殺了你太太。」

「這我認罪。」鬼魂說道：「但這是家務事，跟外人無關。」

「殺人是極大的罪過。」維琪妮雅說。

「我太太既不漂亮，我的衣服也燙不好，而且廚藝奇差。算了，現在說這個也不重要了，事情都過去了。再說，我殺了她，而她的兄弟也把我活活餓死，算是抵銷了。」

「把你餓死？哦，鬼魂先生，不，賽門爵士，你現在肚子餓嗎？我籃子裡有三明治，你想吃嗎？」

「不用了，謝謝，我現在已經不吃東西了。你真好心，不像你那些家人那麼討厭、粗魯、下流、不老實。」

P.44

「你不要這樣說！」維琪妮雅氣得直跺腳，「你才粗魯、討厭、下流！而且你才不老實呢，我知道你偷我箱子裡的顏

料，去塗書房那個可笑的血跡！你先是拿走所有紅色顏料，包括朱紅色，害我沒辦法再畫夕陽，然後你又偷走翠綠色和銘黃色，最後我只剩下靛藍色和鋅白色，我現在只能畫月光，但這種畫看了會讓人心情不好，再說也不怎麼好畫。我雖然沒有告發你，但我心裡很不高興，這整件事實在太荒謬了：有誰聽說過翠綠色的血跡的？」

「你說的倒是。」鬼魂說：「但我能怎麼辦？現在很難弄到真的血，再說是你哥哥起的頭，既然他可以用百落清潔劑，我為什麼不能用你的顏料？」

「晚安了，我要去請爸爸再留雙胞胎弟弟多住一個星期。」

「維琪妮雅小姐請你別走。我這麼寂寞，落落寡歡的，無計可施。我想睡覺，卻無法入眠。」鬼魂叫道。

「哪這麼難啊！你只要躺在床上，把

蠟燭吹熄就可以睡覺了。有時候要保持清醒還不太容易呢，特別是上教堂的時候。睡覺呢，可容易的了，連笨笨的嬰兒都知道怎麼睡覺。」

P.45

「我已經三百年沒有睡過覺了！」他悲傷地說道。維琪妮雅漂亮的藍眼睛聽得睜得大大的。「我三百年沒睡過覺了，好累呀。」

維琪妮雅的表情變得很凝重，顫抖著雙唇。她走到他旁邊，跪下來，望著他年老風霜的臉。「好可憐啊，好可憐的鬼啊，你是不是沒有地方可以睡覺？」她低聲地說道。

睡覺

• 你覺得鬼魂最渴望能做的事是什麼？

他低吟道：「在林子後面那一頭有一個小小的園子，裡頭的草長得又高又密，整晚都可以聽到夜鶯的叫聲，冷月當空，紫杉樹影婆娑，守護著安眠的人。」

維琪妮雅聽得眼裡泛著淚光，用手把臉摀住。

「你說的地方是墓園。」她小聲說道。

「對，是墓園。死亡，一定很美吧。可以躺在柔軟的黃土裡，青草在頭的上方隨風搖曳，享受著寂靜。沒有昨日，沒有明天，沒有歲月，容受生命，一切平靜。你可以幫我，幫我打開死神的門。你有愛神陪你，愛神的力量比死神大。」

P.46

維琪妮雅聽得一陣哆嗦，好半天沒有作聲。她覺得自己好像在做惡夢。

接著鬼魂又開口說話，他的聲音像呼呼的風聲。

「你有看到書房窗戶上寫的那則古老預言嗎？」

「我常看到啊，都背下來了。」小女孩抬眼看著他，大聲說道：「那是用奇怪的黑色字體寫的，很不好讀。總共只有六行：

當黃金般的女孩
能讓罪人說出禱詞
當無果樹結出了果子
當稚子流下眼淚
屋子才會平靜下來
康德維才能永享安寧

但我看不懂是什麼意思。」

鬼魂哀傷地說：「這是說，你會為我的罪孽流下眼淚，因為我自己沒有眼淚；你會為我的靈魂祈禱，因為我沒有信仰；還有，如果你是一個體貼溫柔善良的好人，死亡天使就會垂憐於我。」

P.47

維琪妮雅默不作聲，鬼魂低下頭望著她，她一頭金髮，低著頭，鬼魂看了也不抱希望。這是，她突然站起來，臉色蒼白，眼裡閃爍著奇異的光芒，堅定地說：「我不怕，我去求死亡天使可憐可憐你。」

鬼魂小聲地歡呼了一聲，從椅子上

站了起來。他拉起她的手，用古禮彎下腰親吻了她的手。鬼魂的手指像冰一樣冷，嘴唇卻像火一樣燙，但維琪妮雅任著鬼魂牽著她走過幽暗的房間。

他們一直走到房間的盡頭，鬼魂這時才停下腳步。鬼魂嘴裡唸唸有詞，但維她聽不懂。她把眼睛睜開，卻看到牆壁像煙霧一樣慢慢地散去，眼前出現了一個很大的黑洞，而且襲來一陣冷風，她覺得好像有人在拉她的裙擺。

「快！快！」鬼魂叫道：「不然會來不及。」這時他們身後的牆壁又合了起來，掛毯室裡霎時空無一人。

預言

- 這則預言要如何解讀？
- 你想維琪妮雅和鬼魂去了哪裡？

VI

P. 48

大約十分鐘後，下午茶的搖鈴響了，維琪妮雅卻沒有下樓，歐提斯夫人便差人上樓去找。過了一會兒，僕人回來說到處都找不到小姐。因為維琪妮雅每天傍晚都習慣去花園摘花回來布置餐桌，所以歐提斯夫人

也就沒多操心。然而，等到六點鐘響，還是沒有看到維琪妮雅，歐提斯夫人這時才不安了起來，她叫男孩子們出門去找，她和歐提斯先生則是在家裡仔細搜索每一個房間。

P. 49

到了六點半，男孩子們回到家，說到處都找不到姊姊的蹤跡。這時全家人急得上熱鍋上的螞蟻，不知手措。歐提斯先生吩咐華盛頓和兩個家僕徹底搜索附近區域，然後發電報給全郡的員警，請他們幫忙搜尋。接著他叫人備馬，要妻子和三個兒子坐下來用晚餐，自己則帶著一個僕人沿著亞可路騎去。

P. 50

走沒幾哩路後，歐提斯先生就聽到後面有人騎馬追來的聲音。他轉頭一看，是小柴郡公爵，他騎著小馬追來，滿臉通紅，帽子也沒戴。

「歐提斯先生，很抱歉。」他氣喘吁吁地說：「維琪妮雅不見了，我什麼也吃不下。請別生我的氣，不要叫我回去，我不回去！不要回去！」

公使大人忍不住對這俊俏的年輕人

笑了一下，他對維琪妮雅這麼痴心，讓他很感動。他坐在馬背上，把身體靠過去，輕輕地拍了拍他的肩膀，說道：「這樣吧，塞西爾，如果你不回去，那就跟著我，不過我得在亞可給你找頂帽子。」

「哎呀，還管我的帽子呢！我只要維琪妮雅！」小公爵笑著叫道，然後他們一起奔向火車站。歐提斯先生問站長，有沒有在月台上看到一個長得像維琪妮雅那樣的少女，但都沒有問出什麼消息。

不過站長拍了電報給沿路的車站，保證會加強檢查，協助尋人。歐提斯先生在幫小公爵買了頂帽子之後，便又前往四哩外的貝克雷村莊。他們去找當地的警察，但沒有得到任何線索。他們又騎馬找了一陣子，才策馬回府。回到莊園時，已經十一點左右了，他們累壞了，心情很難過。

P.51

他們看到華盛頓和雙胞胎提著燈籠在路門口等著他們，因為馬路上一片漆黑。維琪妮雅一點消息也沒有。連魚池都撈過了，整個莊園也被翻了一遍，還是沒有任何結果。看米，今晚是找不到維琪妮雅了。歐提斯先生和男孩們很難過地走回屋子裡，僕人則是牽著兩匹馬和公爵的小馬在後面跟著。

他們看到驚慌的僕人們聚在大廳裡，可憐的歐提斯夫人躺在書房的沙發椅上，她心焦如焚，都快瘋掉了，老管家正拿來古龍水擦在她的額頭上。歐提斯先生立刻要夫人一定要吃點什麼，他吩咐下人準備全家的晚餐。這頓晚餐吃得很傷心，大家都不太講話，連雙胞胎都消沉無聲，因為他們很喜歡姊姊。

用完晚餐，歐提斯先生要所有人都上床睡覺，說他們今晚能做的都做了，也不能再做什麼了。他明天一早就會打電報給蘇格蘭警廳，要他們立刻派幾個探長下來。

P.52

維琪妮雅

· 你想維琪妮雅去哪裡了？
· 你曾經鬧過失蹤嗎？
· 當時候別人是如何反應的？

就在他們走出飯廳時，午夜的鐘聲正好響起。當鐘響敲到最後一下的時候，他們聽到一聲爆裂聲和一聲驚叫聲，而且還朝房子打了一聲可怕的雷聲。這時空氣中傳來一陣陰森森的音樂，樓梯口那邊的牆壁忽然砰地一聲，竟開了個洞，從裡頭走出來了臉色灰白的維琪妮雅，她的手裡還拿著一個小盒子。

大家立刻圍上前去，歐提斯夫人緊緊地抱住她，公爵一直猛親著她，雙胞胎在一旁高興得又蹦又跳。

「老天爺！孩子，你去哪裡了呀？」歐提斯先生生氣地問道，還以為她是在跟大家鬧著玩。「我和塞西爾騎著馬到處去找你，你媽都快被你嚇死了。以後再也不許你玩這種遊戲了！」

「是鬼魂搞的鬼！是鬼魂搞的鬼！」雙胞胎一邊跳著，一邊尖聲嚷著。

最後，他們來到一扇大橡木門，維琪妮雅伸手一碰，門就打開了，裡頭是一間低矮的小房間，只有一扇小窗戶。牆上有一個大鐵環，連著鏈子綁住了一副骷髏，骷髏在石板地上伸長著身子，看起來是伸手要去碰旁邊那個曾裝有水的瓶子，和一個曾經裝有食物的盤子，它們都剛好放在他伸手所構不到的地方。

維琪妮雅在骷髏頭旁邊跪了下來，雙手合十，默默地禱告著。其他人很訝異地看著眼前這個可怕的悲劇。鬼魂的祕密終於揭開了。

P.55

「哇！」一個雙胞胎兄弟忽然大喊一聲。原來是他正望著窗外，想弄清楚這個方間的方位。

「哇！那棵老杏樹竟然開花了！月光下可以很清楚地看到花！」

「上帝已經寬恕他了。」維琪妮雅站了起來，口氣嚴肅地說道，有一道美麗的光芒照亮了她的臉龐。

「你真是個天使！」年輕的公爵叫道，然後上前環抱住她的脖子，親吻她。

P.53

「我的心肝寶貝！感謝老天爺啊，你回來了。我再也不許你離開我身邊了。」歐提斯夫人一邊說著，一邊吻著全身顫抖的女兒，用手梳順她打結的金髮。

維琪妮雅小聲地說道：「爸爸，我是和鬼魂在一起。他已經死了，你一定要來看一下。他生前是個壞人，但他已經對自己的所作所為感到後悔，他還在死前給了我這盒美麗的珠寶。」

全家人看著她，驚訝得說不出話來。她表情很正經，然後轉過身帶領大家穿過牆上的洞口，走下一條窄窄的密道，華盛頓拿起桌上的燭臺，跟在後面。

P.56

經過了這些不尋常的事情之後，四天之後，康德維莊園舉行了一場葬禮。

葬禮在夜間十一點開始，靈柩由八匹黑馬拉著，鉛製的棺木上蓋著一塊深紫色的布，布上面用金線繡著康德維家族的盾形紋章。柩車兩邊有家僕舉著火把隨行，場面很隆重。

主祭官是康德維爵士，和維琪妮雅坐在第一輛馬車上。第二輛馬車坐的是美國公使夫婦，接著是華盛頓、雙胞胎和小公爵，最後一輛則是坐著管家溫內太太。大家覺得，溫內太太被鬼魂嚇了五十多年了，應當有資格送他最後一程。

墓園的一角已經挖好一個深穴，就在紫杉樹下，儀式由奧古斯都·鄧波牧師主持，過程很感人。儀式結束之後，家僕依照康德維家族的老古規矩，熄掉手上的火把，然後再把棺木放進墓穴裡。維琪妮雅走上前去，在棺木上放了一個用白色和粉紅色杏花做成的大十字架。

P.57

就在此時，月亮從雲朵後出現，照得寂靜的小墓園一片銀白，遠處的林子裡傳來叢中有一隻夜鶯的啼唱。維琪妮雅想起了鬼魂所描繪的墓園，不禁淚從中來，在返家途中不發一語。

葬禮

· 維琪妮雅在葬禮上是什麼樣的心情？
· 葬禮上的氣氛如何？
· 這個故事的氛圍是如何急轉直下的？

翌日早晨，在康德維爵士返回倫敦之前，歐提斯先生就鬼魂送給維琪妮雅珠寶一事，和康德維爵士商量了一番。這些珠寶非常貴重，特別是那一條古威尼斯款式的紅寶石項鍊，是十六世紀的傑作，價值連城，因此歐提斯先生覺得不能讓女兒接受這份大禮。

P.58

他說：「大人，我也明白貴國的法律，我很清楚，這些珠寶是屬於貴家族的傳家之寶，所以請您將這些珠寶帶回倫敦，就當它們之前是透過奇怪方式被保管下來的財物。至於小女，她只是個孩子，而且我可以驕傲地說，她對於這些東西是不太感興趣的。內人也告訴過我，這些珠寶是極品，如果要賣的話，可以賣到極高價錢。康德維爵士，在這些條件之下，您一定可以諒解，我無論如何都不可能讓任何家人保有這些財物。不過我冒昧一提，維琪妮雅很希望您能夠允許她把盒子留下來，當做是對您那位不幸犯錯的祖先的紀念。由於盒子年代久遠，有點破舊了，您或許會同意她的請求。」

P.59

康德維爵士仔細聆賞著公使一番真誠的話，等歐提斯先生說完之後，他友善地和他握了握手，說道：「敬愛的先生，您那位迷人的小千金，幫我不幸的祖先做了一件大好事，賽門爵士、我和我家族的人都至為感激她莫大的勇氣。這批珠寶本來就是她的，再說，如果我這麼沒良心，把她的東西拿走，那個怪

87

怪的老傢伙沒多久一定會從墳墓裡爬出來，讓我一輩子不得安寧的。至於您提到的傳家之物，只要是遺囑或法律文件上沒有記載的東西，都不能視為傳家之物，這是一批無人知曉的珠寶。我可以向您擔保，我不會比貴府的僕人更有權利持有這些東西。等維琪妮雅小姐長大之後，我敢說她一定會很高興有這些漂亮的東西可以戴。還有，歐提斯先生，您忘了您當初說過的，家具和鬼魂你都會算進莊園的買價裡，所以之前歸鬼魂所有的東西，就由您接手了。」

珠寶

• 你想，歐提斯先生要把珠寶拿給康德維爵士，是正確的做法嗎？為什麼？
• 康德維爵士為什麼又拒絕接受？

P.60

康德維爵士謝絕好意，歐提斯先生很苦惱，要他再三考慮一下，但他態度很堅決，終於說服了公使讓女兒保有鬼魂所贈與的禮物。一八九〇年春天，女王駕臨年輕的柴郡公爵夫人的婚禮，夫人佩戴的珠寶豔驚全場。柴郡公爵一成

年，就和維琪妮雅舉行婚禮。他們郎才女貌，彼此相愛，人人都很高興能見到他們終成眷屬。

蜜月結束之後，公爵夫婦一路來到康德維莊園。隔天下午，他們散步走到松樹林旁邊的那塊寂靜墓園裡。賽門爵士的墓誌銘要寫什麼，當時大家都傷透腦筋，後來決定刻上老先生的名字縮寫，和書房窗戶上的那首詩偈就好。公爵夫人帶來一些美麗的玫瑰花，擺在墳墓上。他們在墓旁靜靜站了一會，然後走進廢棄的舊修道院。

P.61

這時，公爵忽然握住她的手，對她說道：「維琪妮雅，做妻子的不應該對丈夫有所隱瞞。」

「親愛的塞西爾！我從沒有瞞過你什麼！」

「有，你有！」他笑笑地回道：「你沒跟我說過，你和鬼魂鎖在一起的那段時間裡，到底發生了什麼事。」

「塞西爾，這件事我從來也沒有跟別人提過。」維琪妮雅嚴肅地說道。

「我知道，但或許你可以說給我聽聽。」

「請別追問了，塞西爾，我不能說。可憐的賽門爵士，我欠他太多了。真的，別笑，塞西爾。他讓我了解什麼是生命，讓我明白死亡的意義，也讓我知道為什麼生與死都敵不過愛。」

維琪妮雅的祕密

• 你想，為什麼維琪妮雅不肯跟別人說她和鬼魂相處的那一段時間到底發生了什麼事？

• 你想，她跟著鬼魂走了之後，發生了什麼事？

• 你自己有什麼不想跟別人說的祕密嗎？

P. 62

　　公爵站了起來，深情地親吻妻子。

　　「你盡可以守住你的祕密，只要你的心屬於我的就好了。」他呢喃著。

　　「塞西爾，我的心永遠都是你的。」

　　「但以後你會說給我們的孩子聽吧，對吧？」

　　維琪妮雅的臉紅了起來。

ANSWER KEY

Page 9

7

a) US, b) US, c) US, d) UK, e) UK, f) US, g) UK, h) UK

8

a) color

b) centre

c) programme

d) travelling

Page 64

6

The Canterville Ghost

- [a] An old man with clanking chains
- [b] A knight in a suit of armor
- [c] A man in a large hat, a shroud and with a rusty dagger
- [d] A man in a long velvet cloak
- [e] In a long shroud with his jaw tied up and carrying a spade and lantern.

The Otis Family's Reactions

- [1] Mr Otis offers him some Tammany Rising Sun Lubricator.
- [2] The twins throw a pillow at him.
- [1] Mr Otis points his pistol at him.
- [2] The twins shoot pellets from their peashooter at him.
- [3] Mrs Otis offers him Dr Dobell's medicine.
- [1] The twins make a fake ghost to scare him.
- [1] The twins make a butter slide at the top of the stairs.
- [1] The twins jump out and shout at him.
- [2] Washington waits for him with a large water pump.

9

We find out that he killed his wife and that her brothers starved him to death as a punishment.

Page 65

10

Mr Otis doesn't want Virginia to have the jewels because he says that they belong to the Canterville family and that Virginia is too young to have them. Lord Canterville says that Virginia helped the ghost and deserves the jewels. He also says the ghost would be angry if Virginia did not get the jewels and that when the Otis family bought Canterville Chase they also bought its belongings.

11

Length, width and height

12

phantom, specter, spirit

13

They all add to frightening and ghostly atmosphere.

14

Sir Simon is frightened of the ghost. The meeting and his reaction shows his real nature. He is not at all evil and hard.

15

The ghost gets to rest in peace, the family live happily in the house and Virginia marries Cecil.

Page 66

17

- *Lord Canterville*. He sells Canterville Chase to the Otis family.
- *Mrs Umney*. She is the housekeeper of Canterville Chase.
- *The Canterville Ghost*. He was starved to death in the house and has haunted it since then.
- *Cecil*. He is the Duke of Cheshire and is love with Virginia.

18

The Otis Family	Appearance and Character
Hiram B.	Practical, fair
Mrs Otis	Good-looking, nice eyes and profile, full of energy
Washington	Fair-haired, good-looking, good dancer, meticulous
Virginia	Slim, lovely, sweet, sensitive, kind
The twins	Very lively, disrespectful, rude

19

They show the practical, materialistic and non-superstitious nature of Americans.

20

a) Mr Otis, b) Mrs Otis, c) Mr Otis

The words show the Americans' condescending attitude to the British as well as concern with the material world. They all show that a basic lack of communication between the two peoples.

Page 67

21

The words show the ghost to be capable of very ordinary and human emotions and reactions, which are very different to the image he likes to give of himself as being terrible and cruel.

Page 68

26

There is a third-person narrator in the story who comments on the actions and events.

27

a)

Page 69

32

a) 8, b) 2, c) 6, d) 3, e) 7, f)1, g) 10, h) 4, i) 9, j) 5

91

.

國家圖書館出版品預行編目資料

老鬼當家 / Oscar Wilde 著；安卡斯 譯 . 一初版 .
一 [臺北市]：寂天文化，2012.5 面；公分 .

中英對照
ISBN 978-986-184-991-1 (25K 平裝附光碟片)
1. 英語 2. 讀本

805.18 101005986

■作者 _ Oscar Wilde ■改寫 _ David A. Hill ■譯者 _ 安卡斯
■封面設計 _ 蔡怡柔 ■主編 _ 黃鈺云 ■製程管理 _ 蔡智堯 ■校對 _ 陳慧莉
■出版者 _ 寂天文化事業股份有限公司 ■電話 _ 02-2365-9739 ■傳真 _ 02-2365-9835
■網址 _ www.icosmos.com.tw ■讀者服務 _ onlineservice@icosmos.com.tw
■出版日期 _ 2012年5月 初版一刷（250101）
■郵撥帳號 _ 1998620-0 寂天文化事業股份有限公司
■訂購金額600 （含）元以上郵資免費 ■訂購金額600元以下者，請外加郵資60元
■若有破損，請寄回更換 ■版權所有，請勿翻印

Copyright © HELBLING LANGUAGES 2008
This edition has been translated and published under licence
from HELBLING LANGUAGES.
For sale in Taiwan only.
Chinese complex characters translation rights © 2012 by Cosmos Culture Ltd.
All Rights Reserved